MISSING

Look out for more titles
in the MISSING series

When Lightning Strikes
Safe House
Sanctuary

MISSING
Code Name Cassandra

Meg Cabot
Writing as Jenny Carroll

SIMON AND SCHUSTER

SIMON AND SCHUSTER

First published in Great Britain in 2002 by Pocket Books,
an imprint of Simon & Schuster UK Ltd.
Africa House, 64-78 Kingsway, London WC2B 6AH

This edition published in 2004 by Simon & Schuster UK Ltd.
A Viacom Company.

Originally published in the USA in 2001 by Pocket Pulse,
an imprint of Simon & Schuster Inc., New York.

A CIP catalogue record for this book is available
from the British Library upon request.

ISBN 0 689 86092 7

1 3 5 7 9 10 8 6 4 2

Printed by Bookmarque, Croydon, Surrey.

Many thanks to Beth Ader, Jennifer Brown,
John Henry Dreyfuss, Laura Langlie,
Ingrid van der Leeden,
David Walton, and especially Benjamin Egnatz

CHAPTER

1

I don't know why I'm doing this.

Writing this down, I mean. It's not like anybody is making me.

Not this time.

But it seems to me like *somebody* ought to be keeping track of this stuff. Somebody who actually knows what *really* happened.

And it isn't as if you can trust the Feds to do it. Oh, they'll write it down, of course. But they won't get it right.

I just think there needs to be one truthful account. A *factual* one.

So I'm writing it. It isn't a big deal, really. I just hope that someday somebody will actually read it, so I won't feel like it was a complete waste of time . . . not like the majority of my endeavors.

Take, for example, the sign. Now that's a classic example of a wasted endeavor if I ever saw one.

And if you think about it, that's really how it all started. With the sign.

Welcome to Camp Wawasee
Where Gifted Kids Come to Make Sweet Music Together

That's what the sign said.

I know you don't believe me. I know you don't believe that in the history of time, there was ever a sign that said anything that stupid.

But I swear it's true. And I should know: I'm the one who'd painted it.

Don't get me wrong. I didn't *want* to. I mean, they totally made me do it. They handed me the paint and this giant white cotton sheet and told me what to write on it and everything. Their last sign, see, had met with this very tragic accident, in which someone had folded it up and stuck it in the pool house and some noxious chemical had dripped on it and eaten through the fabric.

So they made me make a new one.

It wasn't just that the sign was stupid. I mean, if you got a look at the kids standing under the sign, you'd have known right away that it was also probably libelous. Because if those kids were gifted, I was Jean-Pierre Rampal.

He was this famous flutist, by the way, for those of you who don't know.

Anyway, I had seriously never seen a whinier bunch of kids in my life. And I've been around a lot of kids, thanks to the nature of my, you know, unique gift and all.

But these kids . . . Let me tell you, they were something else. Every last one of them was all, "But I don't *want* to go to music camp," or "Why can't I just stay home with you?" Like the fact that they were going to get to spend six weeks away from their parents was some kind of hardship. If you had told me, at the age of ten or whatever, that I could go somewhere and be away from my parents for six weeks, I'd have been like, "Sign me up, dude."

But not these kids. I suppose on account of the fact they were gifted and all. Maybe gifted kids actually like their parents or something. I wouldn't know.

Still, I tried to believe in the sign. Especially, you know, since I'd made it. Well, with Ruth's help. If you can call Ruth's contribution help, which I wasn't so sure I would. It had consisted mostly of Ruth telling me that my lettering was crooked. Looking at the sign now, I saw that she was right. The letters *were* crooked. But I doubted anyone but me and Ruth had noticed.

"Aren't they cute?"

That was Ruth, sidling up beside me. She was gazing out at the children, looking all dewy-eyed. Apparently she hadn't noticed all the screaming and sniffling and cries of "But I wanna go *home.*"

But I sure had. They were kind of making *me* want to go home, too.

Only, if I went home, I'd be stuck working the steam table. That's how you spend your summers when your parents own a restaurant: working the steam table. There was even less of a chance of escape for me, since my parents own *three* restaurants. It was the least fancy one, Joe Junior's, that offered the buffet of various pasta dishes, all of which were kept warm courtesy of a steam table.

And guess which kid traditionally gets put in charge of the steam table? That's right. The youngest one. Me. It was either that, or the salad bar. And believe me, I had had my fill of deep-sea diving into the ranch dressing tub for stray cherry tomatoes.

But the steam table wasn't the only thing back home that I was trying to avoid.

"I hope I get that one," Ruth gushed, pointing to a cherubic-faced blonde who was standing beneath my sign, clutching a pint-sized cello. "Isn't she sweet?"

"Yeah," I admitted grudgingly. "But what if you get *that* one?"

I pointed to a little boy who was screaming so loudly at the idea of being separated from Mommy and Daddy for a month and a half, he had gone into a full-blown asthma attack. Both of his frenzied-looking parents were thrusting inhalers at him.

"Aw," Ruth said tolerantly. "I was just like that the first year I came here as a camper. He'll be fine by suppertime."

I supposed I had to take her word for it. Ruth's parents had started shipping her off to Camp

Wawasee at the ripe old age of seven, so she had about nine years of experience to draw upon. I, on the other hand, had always spent my summers back at the steam table, bored out of my skull because my best (and pretty much only) friend was gone. In spite of the fact that my parents own three restaurants, in which my friends and I can dine any time we want, I have never exactly been Miss Popularity. This might be on account of the fact that, as my guidance counselor puts it, I have *issues.*

Which was why I wasn't so sure Ruth's idea—of me putting in an application to be a camp counselor—was such a good one. For one thing, despite my special talent, child care is not really my forte. And for another, well, like I said: I have these issues.

But apparently no one noticed my antisocial tendencies during the interview, since I got the job.

"Let me just make sure I got this right," I said to Ruth, as she continued to look longingly at the cellist. "It's Camp Wawasee, Box 40, State Road One, Wawasee, Indiana?"

Ruth wrenched her gaze from Goldilocks.

"For the last time," she said, with some exasperation. "Yes."

"Well," I said with a shrug, "I just wanted to make sure I told Rosemary the right address. It's been over a week since I last got something from her, and I'm a little worried."

"God." Ruth no longer spoke with just *some* exasperation. She was fed up. You could tell. "Would you stop?"

I stuck my chin out. "Stop what?"

"Stop *working*," she said. "You're allowed a vacation once in a while. Jeez."

I went, "I don't know what you're talking about," even though, of course, I did, and Ruth knew it.

"Look," she said. "Everything is going to be all right, okay? I know what to do."

I gave up trying to pretend that I didn't know what she was talking about, and said, "I just don't want to screw it up. Our system, I mean."

Ruth rolled her eyes. "Hello," she said. "What's to screw up? Rosemary sends the stuff to me, I pass it on to you. What, you think after three months of this, I don't have it down yet?"

Alarmed at the volume with which she'd announced this, I grabbed her arm.

"For God's sake, Ruth," I hissed. "Zip it, will you? Just because we're in the middle of nowhere doesn't mean there might not be you-know-whats around. Any one of those doting parents over there could be an F-E-D."

Ruth rolled her eyes again. "Please," was all she said.

She was right, of course: I was overreacting. But there was no denying the fact that Ruth had gotten seriously slack in the discretion department. Basically, since the whole camp thing had been decided, she'd been completely unable to keep anything else in her head. For weeks before we'd left for counselor training, Ruth had kept bubbling, "Aren't you *excited*? Aren't you *psyched*?" Like we were going to Paris with the French Club or something, and not to upstate Indiana to slave away as camp counselors for six weeks. I'd kept wanting to say to her, "Dude, it may not be the steam table, but it's still a *job.*"

I mean, it's not like I don't also have my unofficial part-time career to contend with as well.

The problem was, Ruth's enthusiasm was totally catching. Like, she kept talking about how we were going to spend all of our afternoons on inner tubes, floating along the still waters of Lake Wawasee, getting tan. Or how some of the boy counselors were totally hot, and were going to fall madly in love with us, and offer us rides to the Michigan dunes in their convertibles.

Seriously.

And after a while, I don't know, I just sort of started to believe her.

And that was my second mistake. I mean, after putting in the application in the first place.

Ruth's descriptions of the campers, for instance. Child prodigies, she'd called them. And it's true, you have to audition even to be considered for a place at the camp, both as camper as well as counselor. Ruth's stories about the kids she'd looked after the year before—a cabin full of sensitive, creative, superintelligent little girls, who still wrote her sweet funny letters, a year later—totally impressed me. I don't have any sisters, so when Ruth started in about midnight gossip-and-hair-braiding sessions, I don't know, I began to think, Yeah, okay. This might be for me.

Seriously, I went from, "It's just a job," to "*I* want to escort adorable little girl violinists and flutists to the Polar Bear swim every morning. *I* want to make sure none of them are budding anorexics by monitoring their caloric intake at meals. *I* want to help them decide what to wear the night of the All-Camp Orchestral Concert."

It was like I went mental or something. I couldn't wait to take mastery over the cabin I'd been assigned—Frangipani Cottage. Eight little beds, plus mine in a separate room, in a tiny house (thankfully air-conditioned) that contained a mini-kitchen for snacks and its own private, multiple-showerhead and toilet-stalled bathroom. I had even gone so far as to hang up a sign (with crooked lettering) across the sweet little mosquito-netted front porch that said, *Welcome, Frangipanis!*

Look, I know how it sounds. But Ruth had me whipped up into some kind of camp-counselor frenzy.

But standing there, actually seeing the kids for whom I was going to be responsible for most of July and half of August, I began to have second thoughts. I mean, nobody wants to hang out next to a steam table when it's ninety degrees outside, but at least a steam table can't stick its finger up its nose, then try to hold your hand with that same finger.

It was as I was watching all these kids saying good-bye to their parents, wondering whether I'd just made the worst mistake of my life, that Pamela, the camp's assistant director, came up to me and, clipboard in hand, whispered in my ear, "Can we talk?"

I'll admit it: my heart sped up a little. I figured I was busted. . . .

Because, of course, there was a little something I'd left off of my application for the job. I just hadn't thought it would catch up with me this quickly.

"Uh, sure," I said. Pamela was, after all, my boss. What was I going to say, "Get lost"?

We moved away from Ruth, who was still gazing rapturously at what I would have to say were some very unhappy campers. I swear, I don't think Ruth even noticed how many of those kids were crying.

Then I noticed Ruth wasn't looking at the kids at all. She was staring at one of the counselors, a particularly hot-looking violinist named Todd, who was standing there chatting up some parents. That's when I realized that, in Ruth's head, she wasn't there underneath my crappy sign, watching a bunch of kids shriek, "Mommy, please don't leave me." Not at all. In Ruth's mind, she was in Todd's convertible, heading out toward the dunes for fried perch, a little tartar sauce, and some above-the-waist petting.

Lucky Ruth. She got Todd—at least in her mind's eye—while I was stuck with Pamela, a no-nonsense, khaki-clad woman in her late thirties who was probably about to fire me . . . which would explain why she'd draped an arm sympathetically across my shoulders as we strolled.

Poor Pamela. She was obviously not aware that one of my issues—at least according to Mr. Goodhart, my guidance counselor back at Ernest Pyle High School—is a total aversion to being touched. According to Mr. G, I am extremely sensitive about my personal space, and dislike having it invaded.

Which isn't technically true. There's one person I wouldn't mind invading my personal space.

The problem is, he doesn't do it anywhere near enough.

"Jess," Pamela was saying, as we walked along. She didn't seem to notice the fact that I'd broken into a sweat, on account of my nervousness that I was about to be fired—not to mention trying to restrain myself from flinging her arm off me. "I'm afraid there's been a bit of a change in plans."

A change in plans? That didn't sound, to me, like a prelude to dismissal. Was it possible my secret—which wasn't, actually, much of a secret anymore, but which had apparently not yet reached Pamela's ears—was still safe?

"It seems," Pamela went on, "that one of your fellow counselors, Andrew Shippinger, has come down with mono."

Relieved as I was that our conversation was definitely not going in the "I'm afraid we're going to have to let you go" direction, I have to admit I didn't know what I was supposed to do with this piece of information. The thing about Andrew, I mean. I knew Andrew from my week of counselor training. He played the French horn and was obsessed with

Tomb Raider. He was one of the counselors Ruth and I had rated Undo-able. We had three lists, see: the Undo-ables, like Andrew. The Do-ables, who were, you know, all right, but nothing to get your pulse going.

And then there were the Hotties. The Hotties were the guys like Todd who, like Joshua Bell, the famous violinist, had it all: looks, money, talent . . . and most important of all, a car.

Which was kind of weird. I mean, a car being a prerequisite for hotness. Especially since Ruth has her own car, and it's even a convertible.

But according to Ruth—who was the one who'd made up all these rules in the first place—going to the dunes in your own car simply doesn't count.

The thing is, the chances of a Hottie glancing twice in the direction of either Ruth or me are like nil. Not that we're dogs or anything, but we're no Gwyneth Paltrows.

And that whole Do-able/Undo-able thing? Yeah, need I point out that neither Ruth nor I have ever "done" anybody in our lives?

And I have to say, the way things are going, I don't think it's going to happen, either.

But *Andrew Shippinger?* So not Do-able. Why was Pamela talking to me about him? Did she think *I'd* given him mono? Why do I always get blamed for everything? The only way my lips would ever touch Andrew Shippinger's would be if he sucked down too much water in the pool and needed CPR.

And when was Pamela going to move her arm?

"Which leaves us," she went on, "with a shortage of male counselors. I have plenty of females on my waiting list, but absolutely no more men."

Again, I wondered what this had to do with me. It's true I have two brothers, but if Pamela was thinking either of them would make a good camp counselor, she'd been getting a little too much fresh air.

"So I was wondering," Pamela continued, "if it would upset you very much if we assigned you to the cottage Andrew was supposed to have."

At that point, if she'd asked me to kill her mother, I probably would have said yes. I was that relieved I wasn't being fired—and I'd have done anything, anything at all, to get that arm off me. It isn't just that I have a thing about people touching me. I mean, I do. If you don't know me, keep your damned mitts to yourself. What is the problem there?

But you'd be surprised how touchy-feely these camp people are. It's all trust falls and human pretzel twists to them.

But that wasn't my only problem with Pamela. On top of my other "issues," I have a thing about authority figures. It probably has something to do with the fact that, last spring, one of them tried to shoot me.

So I stood there, sweating copiously, the words "Sure, yeah, whatever, let go of me," already right there on my lips.

But before I could say any of that, Pamela must have noticed how uncomfortable I was with the whole arm thing—either that or she'd realized how damp she was getting from my copious sweating. In any case, she dropped her arm away from me, and suddenly I could breathe easily again.

I looked around, wondering where we were. I'd lost my bearings in my panic over Pamela's touching me. Beneath us lay the gravel path that led to various Camp Wawasee outbuildings. Close by was the dining hall, newly refinished with a twenty-foot ceiling. Next, the camp's administrative offices. Then the infirmary. Beside that, the music building, a modular structure built mostly underground in order to preserve the woodsy feel of the place, with a huge skylight that shone down on a tree-filled atrium from which extended hallways leading to the soundproof classrooms, practice rooms, and so on.

What I couldn't see was the Olympic-sized swimming pool, and the half dozen clay tennis courts. Not that the kids had much time for swimming and tennis, what with all the practicing they had to do for the end-of-session orchestral concert that took place in the outdoor amphitheater, with seating for nine hundred. But nothing was too good for these little budding geniuses. Not far from the amphitheater was the Pit, where campers gathered nightly to link arms and sing while roasting marshmallows around a sunken campfire.

From there the path curved to the various cabins—a dozen for the girls on one side of camp and a dozen for the boys on the other—until it finally sloped down to Camp Wawasee's private lake, in all its mirror-surfaced, tree-lined glory. In fact, the windows of Frangipani Cottage looked out over the lake. From my bed in my little private room, I could see the water without even raising my head.

Only, apparently, it wasn't my bed anymore. I could feel Frangipani Cottage, with its lake views, its angelic flutists, its midnight-gabfest-and-hair-braiding sessions, slipping away, like water down the drain of . . . well, a steam table.

"It's just that, of all our female counselors this year," Pamela was going on, "you really strike me as the one most capable of handling a cabinful of little boys. And you scored so well in your first aid and lifesaving courses—"

Great. I'm being persecuted because of my knowledge of the Heimlich maneuver—honed, of course, from years of working in food services.

"—that I know I can put these kids into your hands and not worry about them a second longer."

Pamela was really laying it on thick. Don't ask me why. I mean, she was my boss. She had every right to assign me to a different cabin if she wanted to. She was the one doling out my paychecks, after all.

Maybe in the past she'd switched a girl counselor to a boys' cabin and gotten flak for it. Like maybe the girl she'd assigned to the cabin had quit or something. I'm not much of a quitter. The fact is, boys would be more work and less fun, but hey, what was I going to do?

"Yeah," I said. The back of my neck still felt damp from where her arm had been. "Well, that's fine."

Pamela reached out to clutch me by the elbow,

looking intently down into my face. Being clutched by the elbow wasn't as bad as having her arm around my shoulders, so I was able to remain calm.

"Do you really mean that, Jess?" she asked me. "You'll really do it?"

What was I going to say, no? And risk being sent home, where I'd have to spend the rest of my summer sweating over trays of meatballs and manicotti at Joe Junior's? And when I wasn't at the restaurant, the only people I'd have to hang around with would be my parents (no thanks); my brother Mike, who was preparing to go away for his first year at Harvard and spent all the time on his computer e-mailing his new roommate, trying to determine who was bringing the minifridge and who was bringing the scanner; or my other brother, Douglas, who did nothing all day but read comic books in his room, coming out only for meals and *South Park*.

Not to mention the fact that for weeks now, there'd been a white van parked across the street from our house that didn't seem to belong to anyone in the neighborhood.

Um, no thanks. I'd stay here, if it was all the same.

"Um, yeah," I said. "Whatever. Just tell me what cabin I'm assigned to now, and I'll start moving my stuff."

Pamela actually hugged me. I can't say a whole lot for her management skills. One thing you would not catch my father doing is hugging one of his employees for agreeing to do what he'd asked her to do.

More like he'd have given her a big fat "so long" if she'd said anything but, "Yes, Mr. Mastriani."

"That's great!" Pamela cried. "That's just great. You are such a doll, Jess."

Yeah, that's me. A regular Barbie.

Pamela looked down at her clipboard. "You'll be in Birch Tree Cottage now."

Birch Tree Cottage. I was giving up frangipani for birch. Story of my damned life.

"Now I'll just have to make sure the alternate can make it tonight." Pamela was still looking down at her chart. "I think she's from your hometown. And she's a flutist, too. Maybe you know her. Karen Sue Hanky?"

I had to bite back a great big laugh. Karen Sue Hanky? Now, if Karen Sue had found out *she* was being reassigned to a boys' cabin, she *definitely* would have cried.

"Yeah, I know her," I said, noncommittally. *Boy, are you making a big mistake*, was what I thought to myself. But I didn't say it out loud, of course.

"She interviewed quite well," Pamela said, still looking down at her clipboard, "but she only scored a five on performance."

I raised my eyebrows. It wasn't news to me, of course, that Karen Sue couldn't play worth a hang. But it seemed kind of wrong for Pamela to be admitting it in front of me. I guess she thought we were friends and all, on account of me not crying when she told me she was moving me to a boys' cabin.

The thing is, though, I already have all the friends I can stand.

"And she's only fourth chair," Pamela murmured, looking down at her chart. Then she heaved this enormous sigh. "Oh, well," she said. "What else can we do?"

Pamela smiled down at me, then started back to the administrative offices. She had apparently forgotten the fact that I am only third chair, just one up from Karen Sue.

My performance audition score, however, for the camp had been ten. Out of ten.

Oh, yeah. I rock.

Well, at playing the flute, anyway. I don't actually rock at much else.

I figured I'd better get a move on, if I was going to gather my stuff before any of the Frangipanis showed up and got the wrong idea . . . like that Camp Wawasee was unorganized or something. Which, of course, they were, as both the disaster with the sign—the one I told you about earlier—and the fact that they'd hired me attested to. I mean, had they even run my name through Yahoo!, or anything? If they had, they might have gotten an unpleasant little surprise.

Skirting the pack of friendly—a little *too* friendly, if you ask me; you had to shove them out of your way with your knees to escape their long, hot tongues—dogs that roamed freely around the camp, I headed back to Frangipani Cottage, where I began throwing my stuff into the duffel bag I'd brought it all in. It burned me up a little to think that Karen Sue Hanky was the one who was going to get to enjoy that excellent view of Lake Wawasee from what had been my bed. I'd known Karen Sue since kindergarten, and if anyone had ever suffered from a case of the I'm-So-Greats, it was Karen Sue. Seriously. The girl totally thought she was all that, just because her dad owned the biggest car dealership in town, she happened to be blonde, and she played fourth chair flute in our school orchestra.

And yeah, you had to audition to make the Symphonic Orchestra, and yeah, it had won all these awards and was mostly made up of only juniors and seniors, and Karen and I had both made it as sophomores, but please. I ask you, in the vast spectrum of things, is fourth chair in Symphonic Orchestra anything? Anything at all? Not. So not.

Not to Karen it wasn't, though. She would never rest until she was first chair. But to get there, she had to challenge and beat the person in third chair.

Yeah. Me.

And I can tell you, that was so not going to happen. Not in this world. I wouldn't call making third chair of Ernest Pyle High School's Symphonic Orchestra a world-class accomplishment, or anything, but it wasn't something I was going to let Karen Sue take away from me. No way.

Not like she was taking Frangipani Cottage away from me.

Well, frangipani, I decided, was a stupid plant,

anyway. Smelly. A big smelly flower. Birch trees were way better.

That's what I told myself, anyway.

It wasn't until I actually got to Birch Tree Cottage that I changed my mind. Okay, first off, can I just tell you what a logistical nightmare it was going to be, supervising eight little boys? How was I even going to be able to take a shower without one of them barging in to use the john, or worse, spying on me, as young boys—and some not so young ones, as illustrated by my older brothers, who spend inordinate amounts of time gazing with binoculars at Claire Lippman, the girl next door—are wont to do?

Plus Birch Tree Cottage was the farthest cabin from everything—the pool, the amphitheater, the music building. It was practically in the *woods*. There was no lake view here. There was not even any light here, since the thickly leafed tree branches overhead let in not the slightest hint of sun. Everything was damp and smelled faintly of mildew. There *was* mildew in the showers.

Let me be the first to tell you: Birch Tree Cottage? Yeah, it sucked.

I missed Frangipani Cottage, and the little girls whose hair I could have been French braiding, already. If I knew how to French braid, that is.

Still, maybe they could have taught me. My little girl campers, I mean.

And when I'd stowed my stuff away and stepped outside the cabin and saw the first of my charges heading toward me, lugging their suitcases and instruments behind them, I missed Frangipani Cottage even more.

I'm serious. You never saw a scruffier, more sour-faced group of kids in your life. Ranging in age from ten to twelve years old, these were no mischievous-but-good-at-heart Harry Potters.

Oh, no.

Far from it.

These kids looked exactly like what they were: spoiled little music prodigies whose parents couldn't wait to take a six-week vacation from them.

The boys all stopped when they saw me and stood there, blinking through the lenses of their glasses, which were fogged up on account of the humidity. Their parents, who were helping them with their luggage, looked like they were longing to get as far from Camp Wawasee as they possibly could—preferably to a place where pitchers of margaritas were being served.

I hastened to say the speech I'd been taught at counselor training. I remembered to substitute the words *birch tree* for *frangipani.*

"Welcome to Birch Tree Cottage," I said. "I'm your counselor, Jess. We're going to have a lot of fun together."

The parents, you could tell, couldn't care less that I wasn't a boy. They seemed pleased by the fact that I clearly bathed regularly and could speak English.

The boys, however, looked shocked. Sullen and shocked.

One of them went, "Hey, you're a *girl.*"

Another one wanted to know, "What's a girl counselor doing in a boys' cabin?"

A third one said, "She's not a girl. Look at her hair," which I found highly insulting, considering the fact that my hair isn't *that* short.

Finally, the most sullen-looking boy of them all, the one with the mullet cut and the weight problem, went, "She is, too, a girl. She's that girl from TV. The lightning girl."

And with that, my cover was blown.

CHAPTER

2

That was me. Lightning Girl. The girl from TV.

Lucky me. Lucky, lucky, *lucky* me. Could there *be* a girl luckier than me? I don't think so. . . .

Oh, wait—I know. How about some girl who *hadn't* been struck by lightning and developed weird psychic powers overnight? Hey, yeah. *That* girl might be luckier than me. That girl might be *way* luckier than me. Don't you think?

I looked down at Mullet Head. Actually, not that much down, because he was about as tall as I was—which isn't saying much, understand.

Anyway, I looked down at him, and I went, "I don't know what you're talking about."

Just like that. Real smooth, you know? I'm telling you, I had it on.

But it didn't matter. It didn't matter at all.

One of the boys, a skinny one clutching a trumpet

case, said, "Hey, yeah, you *are* that girl. I remember you. You're the one who got hit by lightning and got all those special powers!"

The other boys exchanged excited glances. The glances clearly said, *Cool. Our counselor's a mutant.*

One of them, however, a dark, delicate-looking boy who had no parents with him and spoke with a slight accent, asked shyly, "What special powers?"

The chubby boy with the unfortunate haircut—a mullet, short in front and long in back—who'd outed me in the first place smacked the little dark boy in the shoulder, hard. The chubby boy's mother, from whom it appeared he'd inherited his current gravitationally challenged condition, did not even tell him to knock it off.

"What do you mean, what special powers?" Mullet Head demanded. "Where have you been, retard? On the little bus?"

All of the other boys chuckled at this witticism. The dark little boy looked stricken.

"No," he said, clearly puzzled by the little bus reference. "I come from French Guiana."

"Guiana?" Mullet Head seemed to find this hilarious. "Is that anywhere near Gonorrhea?"

Mrs. Mullet Head, to my astonishment, laughed at this witticism.

That's right. Laughed.

Mullet Head, I could see, was going to be what Pamela had referred to during counselor training as a challenge.

"I'm sorry," I said sweetly to him. "I know I look

like that girl who was on TV and all, but it wasn't me. Now, why don't you all go ahead and—"

Mullet Head interrupted me. "It was, *too*, you," he declared with a scowl.

Mrs. Mullet Head went, "Now, Shane," in this tone that showed she was proud of the fact that her son was no pushover. Which was true. Shane wasn't a pushover. What he was, clearly, was a huge pain in the—

"Um," another one of the parents said. "Hate to interrupt, but do you mind if we go ahead and go inside, miss? This tuba weighs a ton."

I stepped aside and allowed the boys and their parents to enter the cabin. Only one of them paused as he went by me, and that was the little French Guianese boy. He was lugging an enormous and very expensive-looking suitcase. I could see no sign of an instrument.

"I am Lionel," he said gravely.

Only he didn't pronounce it the way we would. He pronounced it Lee-Oh-Nell, with the emphasis on the *Nell*.

"Hey, Lionel," I said, making sure I pronounced it properly. We'd been warned at counselor training that there'd be a lot of kids from overseas, and that we should do all we could to show that Camp Wawasee was cultural-diversity aware. "Welcome to Birch Tree Cottage."

Lionel flashed me another glimpse of those pearly whites, then continued lugging his big heavy bag inside.

I decided to let the boys and their parents slug it out on their own, so I stayed where I was out on the mosquito-netted porch, listening to the ruckus inside as the kids tore around, choosing beds. Off in the distance, I saw someone else wearing the camp counselor uniform—white collared short-sleeve shirt with blue shorts—standing on his porch, looking in my direction. Whoever he was lifted a hand and waved.

I waved back, even though I didn't have any idea who it was. Hey, you never knew. He might have owned a convertible.

It took about two minutes for the first fight to break out.

"No, it's mine!" I heard someone inside the cabin shriek in anguish.

I stalked inside. All of the beds—thankfully, not bunks—had belongings strewn across them. The fight was evidently not territorial in nature. Little boys do not apparently care much about views, and thankfully know nothing about feng shui.

The fight was over a box of Fiddle Faddle, which Shane was holding and Lionel evidently wanted.

"It is *mine!*" Lionel insisted, making a leap for the box of candy. "Give it back to me!"

"If you don't have enough to share," Shane said primly, "you shouldn't have brought it in the first place."

Shane was so much bigger than Lionel that he didn't even have to hold the box very high in the air to keep it out of the smaller boy's reach. He just had to hold it at shoulder level. Lionel, even standing on his tiptoes, wasn't tall enough to grab it.

Meanwhile, Shane's mother was just standing there with a little smile on her face, carefully unpacking the contents of her boy's suitcase and placing each item in the drawers in the platform beneath her son's mattress.

The rest of the boys, however, and quite a few of the parents, were watching the little drama unfolding in Birch Tree Cottage with interest.

"Didn't they ever teach you," Shane asked Lionel, "about sharing back in Gonorrhea?"

I knew rapid and decisive action was necessary. I could not do what I'd have liked to do, which was whop Shane upside the head. Pamela and the rest of the administrative staff at Camp Wawasee had been very firm on the subject of corporal punishment—they were against it. That was why they'd spent four hours of one of our training days going over appropriate versus inappropriate disciplinary action. Whopping campers upside the head was expressly forbidden.

Instead, I stepped forward and snatched the box of Fiddle Faddle out of Shane's hand.

"There is no," I declared loudly, "outside food of any kind allowed in Birch Tree Cottage. The only food anyone may bring into this cabin is food from the dining hall. Is that understood?"

Everyone stood staring at me, some in consternation. Shane's mother looked particularly shocked.

"Well, that sure is a change from last year," she

said, in a voice that was too high-pitched and sugary to come from a woman who had produced, as she had, the spawn of Satan. "Last year, the boys could have all the candy and cookies from home they wanted. That's why I packed this."

Shane's mother hauled up another suitcase and flung it open to reveal what looked like the entire contents of a 7-Eleven candy rack. The other boys gathered around, their eyes goggling at the sight of so many Nestlé, Mars, and Hershey's products.

"Contraband," I said, pointing into the suitcase. "Take it home with you, please."

The boys let out a groan. Mrs. Shane's many chins began to tremble.

"But Shane gets hungry," she said, "in the middle of the night—"

"I will make sure," I said, "that there are plenty of healthful snacks for all the boys."

I was, of course, making up the rule about outside food. I just didn't want to have to be breaking up fights over Fiddle Faddle every five minutes.

As if sensing my thoughts, Shane's mother looked at the box in my hand.

"Well, what about that?" she demanded, pointing at it. "You can't send that home with *his* parents—" The accusing finger swung in Lionel's direction. "They didn't bother coming."

Uh, because they live in *French Guiana*, I wanted to say to her. Hello?

Instead, I found myself saying possibly the stupidest thing of all time: "This box of Fiddle Faddle will remain in my custody until camp is over, at which point, I will return it to its rightful owner."

"Well," Shane's mother sniffed. "If Shane can't have any candy, I don't think the other boys should be allowed any, either. I hope you intend to search their bags, as well."

Which was how, by the time supper rolled around, I had five boxes of Fiddle Faddle, two bags of Double-Stuff Oreo cookies, a ten-pack of Snickers bars, two bags of Fritos and one of Doritos, seven Gogurts in a variety of flavors, one bag of Chips Ahoy chocolate chip cookies, a box of Count Chocula, a two-pound bag of Skittles, and a six-pack of Yoo-Hoo locked in my room. The parents, thankfully, had left, chased off the property by the sound of the dinner gong. The good-byes were heartfelt but, except on the part of Shane's mother, not too tearful. Somewhere out there, a lot of champagne corks were popping.

As soon as the last parent had departed, I informed the boys that we were headed to the dining hall, but that before we went, I wanted to make sure I had all their names down. Once that was settled, I told them, I'd teach them the official Birch Tree Cottage song.

Shane and Lionel I was already well acquainted with. The skinny kid who played trumpet turned out to be called John. The tuba player was Arthur. We had two violinists, Sam and Doo Sun, and two pianists, Tony and Paul. They were pretty much all your typical gifted musician types—pasty-skinned, prone to aller-gies, and way too smart for their own good.

"How come," John wanted to know, "you told us you aren't that girl from TV, when you totally are?"

"Yeah," Sam said. "And how come you can only find missing kids with your psychic powers? How come you can't find cool stuff, like gold?"

"Or the remote control." Arthur, I could already tell, was going to make up for his unfortunate name by being the cabin comedian.

"Look," I said. "I told you. I don't know what you guys are talking about. I just look like that lightning girl, okay? It wasn't me. Now—" I felt a change of subject was in order. "Shane, you haven't told us yet what instrument you play."

"The skin flute," Shane said. All of the boys but Lionel cracked up.

"Really?" Lionel looked shyly pleased. "I play the flute, too."

Shane shrieked with laughter upon hearing this. "You would!" he cried. "Being from Gonorrhea!"

Now that his mother was gone, I felt free to walk over and flick the top of Shane's ear with my middle finger hard enough to produce a very satisfying snapping noise. One of my other issues, on which I'd promised Mr. Goodhart to work during my summer vacation, was a tendency to take out my frustrations with others in a highly physical manner—a fact because of which I had spent most of my sophomore year in detention.

"Ow!" Shane cried, shooting me an indignant look. "What'd you do *that* for?"

"While you are living in Birch Tree Cottage," I

informed him—as well as the rest of the boys, who were staring at us—"you will conduct yourself as a gentleman, which means you will refrain from making overtly sexual references within my hearing. Additionally, you will not insult other people's countries of origin."

Shane's face was a picture of confusion. "Huh?" he said.

"No sex talk," John translated for him.

"Aw." Shane looked disgusted. "Then how am I supposed to have any fun?"

"You will have good, clean fun," I informed him. "And that's where the official Birch Tree Cottage song comes in."

And then, while we undertook the long walk to the dining hall, I taught them the song.

> *I met a miss,*
> *She had to pi—*
> *—ck a flower.*
> *Stepped in the grass,*
> *up to her a—*
> *—nkle tops.*
> *She saw a bird,*
> *stepped on a tur—*
> *—key feather.*
> *She broke her heart,*
> *and let a far—*
> *—mer carry her home.*

"See?" I said as we walked. We had the longest walk of anyone to the dining hall, so by the time we'd reached it, the boys had the song entirely memorized. "No dirty words."

"Almost dirty," Doo Sun said with relish.

"That's the stupidest song I ever heard," Shane muttered. But I noticed he was singing it louder than anyone as we entered the dining hall. None of the other cabins, we soon learned, had official songs. The residents of Birch Tree Cottage sang theirs with undisguised gusto as they picked up their trays and got into the concession line.

I spied Ruth sitting with the girls from her cabin. She waved to me. I sauntered over.

"What is going on?" Ruth wanted to know. "What are you doing with all those boys?"

I explained the situation. When she had heard all, Ruth's mouth fell open and she went, her blue eyes flashing behind her glasses, "That is so unfair!"

"It'll be all right," I said.

"What will?" Shelley, a violinist and one of the other counselors, came by with a tray loaded down with chili fries and Jell-O.

Ruth told her what had happened. Shelley looked outraged.

"That is *bull*," she said. "A boys' cabin? How are you going to take a shower?"

Seeing everyone else so mad on my behalf, I started feeling less bad about the whole thing. I shrugged and said, "It won't be so bad. I'll manage."

"I know what you can do," Shelley said. "Just shower at the pool, in the girls' locker room."

"Or one of the guys from the cabins near yours can keep your campers occupied," Ruth said. "I mean, it wouldn't kill Scott or Dave to take on some extra kids for half an hour, here and there."

"What won't kill us?" Scott, an oboe player with thick glasses who'd nevertheless been judged Do-able thanks to his height (a little over six feet) and thighs (muscular) came over, followed closely by his shadow, a stocky Asian trumpet player named Dave . . . also rated Do-able, courtesy of a set of sur-prisingly washboard abs.

"They reassigned Jess to a boys' cabin," Shelley informed them.

"No kidding?" Scott looked interested. "Which one?"

"Birch," I said carefully.

Scott and Dave exchanged enthusiastic glances.

"Hey," Scott cried. "That's right near us! We're neighbors!"

"That was you?" Dave grinned down at me. "Who waved at me?"

"Yeah," I said. But you waved first.

I didn't say that part out loud, though. I won-dered if either Dave or Scott had a convertible. I doubted it.

Not that I cared. I was taken, anyway. Well, in my opinion, at least.

"Don't worry, Jessica," Dave said, with a wink. "We'll look after you."

Just what I needed. To be looked after by Scott and Dave. Whoopee.

Ruth speared a piece of lettuce. She was eating a salad, as usual. Ruth would starve herself all summer in order to look good in a bikini she would never quite work up the courage to wear. If Scott or Dave or, well, anybody, for that matter, did ask her to go with him to the dunes, she would go dressed in a T-shirt and shorts that she would not remove, even in the event of heat stroke.

Ruth eyed me over a forkful of romaine. "What was with that dirty song you had those guys singing when you all came in?"

"It wasn't dirty," I said.

"It sounded dirty." Scott, who'd taken a seat on Ruth's other side, instead of sitting with his cabin, like he was supposed to, was eating spaghetti and meatballs. He was doing it wrong, too, cutting the pasta up into little bite-sized portions, instead of twirling it on his fork. My dad would have had an embolism.

Scott, I decided, must like Ruth. I knew Ruth liked Todd, the hot-looking violinist, but Scott wasn't such a bad guy. I hoped she'd give him a chance. Oboe players are generally better humored than violinists.

"Technically," I said, "that song wasn't a bit dirty."

"Oh, God," Ruth said, making a face at something she'd spotted over my shoulder. "What's *she* doing here?"

I looked around. Standing behind me was Karen Sue Hanky. I hadn't seen Karen Sue since school had let out for the summer, but she looked much the same as she always did—rat-faced and full of herself.

She was holding a tray laden with grains and legumes. Karen Sue is vegan.

Then I noticed that beside Karen Sue stood Pamela.

"Excuse me, Jess?" Pamela said. "Can I see you for a moment in my office, please?"

I shot Karen Sue a dirty look. She simpered back at me.

This was going to be, I realized, a long summer.

In more ways than one.

CHAPTER

3

"It wasn't dirty," I said as I followed Pamela into her office.

"I know," Pamela said. She collapsed into the chair behind her desk. "But it sounds dirty. We've had complaints."

"Already?" I was shocked. "From who?"

But I knew. Karen Sue, on top of the whole vegan thing, is this total prude.

"Look," I said, "if it's that much of a problem, I'll tell them they can't sing it anymore."

"Fine. But to tell you the truth, Jess," Pamela said, "that's not really why I called you in here."

All of a sudden, it felt as if someone had poured the contents of a Big Gulp down my back.

She knew. Pamela *knew.*

And I hadn't even seen it coming.

"Look," I said. "I can explain."

"Oh, can you?" Pamela shook her head. "I suppose it's partly our fault. I mean, how the fact that you're *the* Jessica Mastriani slipped through our whole screening process, I cannot imagine. . . ."

Visions of steam tables danced in my head.

"Listen, Pamela." I said it low, and I said it fast. "That whole thing—the getting struck by lightning thing? Yeah, well, it's true. I mean I was struck by lightning and all. And for a while, I did have these special powers. Well, one, anyway. I mean, I could find lost kids and all. But that was it. And the thing is—well, as you probably know—it went away."

I said this last part very loudly, just in case my old friends, Special Agents Johnson and Smith, had the place bugged or whatever. I hadn't noticed any white vans parked around the campgrounds, but you never knew. . . .

"It went away?" Pamela was looking at me nervously. "Really?"

"Uh-huh," I said. "The doctors told me it probably would. You know, after the lightning was done rattling around in me and all." At least, that was how I liked to think about it. "And it turned out they were right. I am now totally without psychic power. So, um, there's really nothing for you to worry about, so far as negative publicity for the camp, or hordes of reporters descending on you, or anything like that. The whole thing is totally over."

Not even remotely true, of course, but what Pamela didn't know couldn't, I figured, hurt her.

"Don't get me wrong, Jess," she said. "We love

having you here—especially with you being so good about changing cabins—but Camp Wawasee has never known a single hint of controversy in the fifty years it's been in existence. I'd hate for . . . well, anything *untoward* to happen while you're here. . . ."

Untoward was, I guess, Pamela's way of referring to what had happened last spring, after I'd been struck by lightning and then got "invited" to stay at Crane Military for a few days, while some scientists studied my brain waves and tried to figure out how it was that, just by showing me a picture of a missing person, I could wake up the next morning knowing exactly where that person was.

Unfortunately, after they'd studied it for a while, the people at Crane had decided that my newfound talent might come in handy for tracking down so-called traitors and other unsavory individuals who really, as far as I knew, didn't want to be found. And while I'm as anxious as anybody to incarcerate serial killers and all, I just figured I'd stick to finding missing kids . . . specifically, kids who actually want to be found.

Only the people at Crane had turned out to be surprisingly unhappy to hear this.

But after some friends of mine and I had broken some windows and cut through some fencing and, oh, yeah, blown up a helicopter, they came around. Well, sort of. It helped, I guess, that I called the press and told them I couldn't do it anymore. Find missing people, I mean. That little special talent of mine just dried up and blew away. *Poof.*

That's what I told them, anyway.

But you could totally see where Pamela was coming from. On account of the fireball caused by the exploding helicopter and all. It *had* made a lot of papers. You don't get fireballs every day. At least, not in Indiana.

Pamela frowned a little. "The thing is, Jess," she said, "even though, as you say, you no longer have, um, any psychic powers, I have heard . . . well, I've heard missing kids across the country are still sort of, um, turning up. A lot more kids than ever turned up before . . . well, before your little weather-related accident. And thanks to some"—she cleared her throat—"anonymous tips."

My winning smile didn't waver.

"If that's true," I said, "it sure isn't because of me. No, ma'am. I am officially retired from the kid-finding business."

Pamela didn't exactly look relieved. She looked sort of like someone who wanted—really, really wanted—to believe something, but didn't think she should. Kind of like a kid whose friends had told her Santa Claus doesn't exist, but whose parents were still trying to maintain the myth.

Still, what could she do? She couldn't sit there and call me a liar to my face. What proof did she have?

Plenty, as it turned out. She just didn't know it.

"Well," she said. Her smile was as stiff as the Welcome to Camp Wawasee sign had been, in the places it hadn't been eaten away. "All right, then. I guess . . . I guess that's that."

I got up to go, feeling a little shaky. Well, you would have felt shaky, too, if you'd have come as close as I had to spending the rest of the summer stirring steaming platters of rigatoni bolognese.

"Oh," Pamela said, as if remembering something. "I almost forgot. You're friends with Ruth Abramowitz, aren't you? This came for her the other day. It didn't fit into her mailbox. Could you hand it to her? I saw you sitting with her at dinner just now. . . ."

Pamela took a large padded envelope out from behind her desk and handed it to me. I stood there, looking down at it, my throat dry.

"Um," I said. "Sure. Sure, I'll give it to her."

My voice sounded unusually hoarse. Well, and why not? Pamela didn't know it, of course, but what she'd just given me—its contents, anyway—could prove that every single thing I'd just told her was an out-and-out lie.

"Thanks," Pamela said with a tired smile. "Things have just been so hectic . . ."

The corners of my mouth started to ache on account of how hard I was still smiling, pretending like I wasn't upset or anything. I should, I knew, have taken that envelope and run. That's what I should have done. But something made me stay and go, still in that hoarse voice, "Can I ask you a question, Pamela?"

She looked surprised. "Of course you can, Jess."

I cleared my throat, and kept my gaze on the strong, loopy handwriting on the front of the envelope. "Who told you?"

Pamela knit her eyebrows. "Told me what?"

"You know. About me being the lightning girl." I looked up at her. "And that stuff about how kids are still being found, even though I'm retired."

Pamela didn't answer right away. But that was okay. I knew. And I hadn't needed any psychic powers to tell me, either. Karen Sue Hanky was dead meat.

It was right then there was a knock on Pamela's office door. She yelled, "Come in," looking way relieved at the interruption.

This old guy stuck his head in. I recognized him. He was Dr. Alistair, the camp director. He was kind of red in the face, and he had a lot of white hair that stuck out all around his shining bald head. He was supposedly this very famous conductor, but let me ask you: If he's so famous, what's he doing running what boils down to a glorified band camp in northern Indiana?

"Pamela," he said, looking irritated. "There's a young man on the phone looking for one of the counselors. I told him that we are not running an answering service here, and that if he wants to speak to one of our employees, he can leave a message like everybody else and we will post it on the message board. But he says it's an emergency, and—"

I moved so fast, I almost knocked over a chair.

"Is it for me? Jess Mastriani?"

It wasn't any psychic ability that told me that phone call was probably for me. It was the combination of the words "young man" and "emergency." All of the young men of my acquaintance, when confronted by someone like Dr. Alistair, would definitely go for the word "emergency" as soon as they heard about that stupid message board.

Dr. Alistair looked surprised . . . and not too pleased.

"Why, yes," he said. "If your name is Jessica, then it is for you. I hope Pamela has explained to you the fact that we are not running a message service here, and that the making or receiving of personal calls, except during Sunday afternoons, is expressly—"

"But it's an *emergency*," I reminded him.

He grimaced. "Down the hall. Phone at the reception desk. Press line one."

I was out of Pamela's office like a shot.

Who, I wondered, as I jogged down the hall, could it be? I knew who I *wanted* it to be. But the chances of Rob Wilkins calling me were slim to none. I mean, he never calls me at home. Why would he call me at camp?

Still, I couldn't help hoping Rob had overcome this totally ridiculous prejudice he's got against me because of my age. I mean, so what if he's eighteen and has graduated already, while I still have two years of high school left? It's not like he's leaving town to go to college in the fall, or something. Rob's not going to college. He has to work in his uncle's garage and support his mother, who recently got laid off from the factory she had worked in for like twenty years or something. Mrs. Wilkins was having trouble finding another job, until I suggested food services and gave her the number at Joe's. My dad, without even knowing Mrs. Wilkins and I were acquainted, hired her and put her on days at Mastriani's—which isn't a bad shift at all. He saves the totally crappy jobs and shifts for his kids. He believes strongly in teaching us what he calls a "work ethic."

But when I got to the phone and pushed line one, it wasn't Rob. Of course it wasn't Rob. It was my brother Douglas.

And that's how I *really* knew it wasn't an emergency. If it had been an emergency, it would have been *about* Douglas. The only emergencies in our family are because of Douglas. At least, they have been, ever since he got kicked out of college on account of these voices in his head that are always telling him to do stuff, like slit his wrists, or stick his hand in the barbecue coals. Stuff like that.

But so long as he takes his medicine, he's all right. Well, all right for Douglas, which is kind of relative.

"Jess," he said, after I went, "Hello?"

"Oh, hey." I hoped my disappointment that it was Douglas and not Rob didn't show in my voice.

"How's it going? Who was that freak who answered the phone? Is that your boss, or something?"

Douglas sounded good. Which meant he'd been taking his medication. Sometimes he thinks he's cured, so he stops. That's when the voices usually come back again.

"Yeah," I said. "That was Dr. Alistair. We aren't

supposed to get personal calls, except on Sunday afternoons. Then it's okay."

"So he explained to me." Douglas didn't sound in the least bit ruffled by his conversation with Dr. Alistair, world-famous orchestra conductor. "And you prefer working for him over Dad? At least Dad would let you get phone calls at work."

"Yeah, but Dad would withhold my pay for the time I spent on the phone."

Douglas laughed. It was good to hear him laugh. He doesn't do it very often anymore.

"He would, too," he said. "It's good to hear your voice, Jess."

"I've only been gone a week," I reminded him.

"Well, a week's a long time. It's seven days. Which is one hundred and sixty-eight hours. Which is ten thousand, eighty minutes. Which is six hundred thousand, four hundred seconds."

It wasn't the medication that was making Douglas talk like this. It wasn't even his illness. Douglas has always gone around saying stuff like this. That's why, in school, he'd been known as The Spaz, and Dorkus, and other, even worse names. If I'd asked him to, Douglas could tell me exactly how many seconds it would be before I got back home. He could do it without even thinking about it.

But go to college? Drive a car? Talk to a girl to whom he wasn't related? No way. Not Douglas.

"Is that why you called me, Doug?" I asked. "To tell me how long I've been gone?"

"No." Douglas sounded offended. Weird as he is,

he doesn't think he's the least unusual. Seriously. To Douglas, he's just, you know, average.

Yeah. Like your average twenty-year-old guy just sits around in his bedroom reading comic books all day long. Sure.

And my parents let him! Well, my mom, anyway. My dad's all for making Doug work the steam table in my absence, but Mom keeps going, "But Joe, he's still *recovering*. . . ."

"I called," Douglas said, "to tell you it's gone."

I blinked. "What's gone, Douglas?"

"You know," he said. "That van. The white one. That's been parked in front of the house. It's gone."

"Oh," I said, blinking some more. "*Oh.*"

"Yeah," Douglas said. "It left the day after you did. And you know what that means."

"I do?"

"Yeah." And then, I guess because it was clear to him that I wasn't getting it, he elaborated. "It proves that you weren't being paranoid. They really *are* still spying on you."

"Oh," I said. "Wow."

"Yeah," Douglas said. "And that's not all. Remember how you told me to let you know if anyone we didn't know came around, asking about you?"

I perked up. I was sitting at the receptionist's desk in the camp's administrative offices. The receptionist had gone home for the day, but she'd left behind all her family photos, which were pinned up all around her little cubicle. She must have really liked NASCAR racing, because there were a lot of photos of guys in these junky-looking race cars.

"Yeah? Who was it?"

"I don't know. He just called."

Now I really perked up. Rob. It had to have been Rob. My family didn't know about him, on account of how I never really told them we were going out. Because we aren't, technically. Going out. For the reasons I already told you. So what's to tell?

Plus my mom would so kill me if she knew I was seeing a guy who wasn't, you know, college-bound. And had a police record.

"Yeah?" I said eagerly. "Did he leave a message?"

"Naw. Just asked if you were home, is all."

"Oh." Now that I thought about it, it probably hadn't been Rob at all. I mean, I'd made this total effort to let Rob know I was leaving for the rest of the summer. I had even gone to his uncle's garage, you know, where Rob works, and had this long conversation with his feet while he'd been underneath a Volvo station wagon, about how I was going away for seven weeks and this was his last chance to say good-bye to me, et cetera.

But had he looked the least bit choked up? Had he begged me not to go? Had he given me his class ring or an ID bracelet or something to remember him by? Not. So not. He'd come out from under that Volvo and said, "Oh, yeah? Well, that'll be good for you, to get away for a while. Hand me that wrench right there, will you?"

I tell you, romance is dead.

"Was it a Fed?" I asked Douglas.

Douglas went, "I don't know, Jess. How am I supposed to know that? He sounded like a guy. You know. Just a guy."

I grunted. That's the thing about Feds, see. They can sound just like normal people. When they aren't wearing their trench coats and earpieces, they look just like anybody else. They're not like the Feds on TV—you know, like Mulder and Scully, or whatever. Like, they aren't really handsome, or pretty, or anything. They just look . . . average. Like the kind of people you wouldn't actually notice, if they were following you—or even if they were standing right next to you.

They're tricky that way.

"That was it?" I noticed that there was this one guy who kept reappearing in the photographs on the secretary's bulletin board. He was probably her boyfriend or something. A NASCAR-driver boyfriend. I felt jealous of the secretary. The guy she liked liked her back. You could tell by the way he smiled into the camera. I wondered what it would be like to have the boy you like like you back. Probably pretty good.

"Well, not really," Douglas said. He said it in this way that—well, I could just tell I wasn't going to like the rest of this story.

"What," I said flatly.

"Look," Douglas said. "He sounded . . . well, he seemed to really want to talk to you. He said it was really important. He kept asking when you'd be back."

"You didn't," I said, just as flatly.

"He kept asking and asking," Douglas said. "Finally I had to say you wouldn't be back for six weeks, on account of you were up at Lake Wawasee. Look, Jess, I know I screwed up. Don't be mad. Please don't be mad."

I wasn't mad. How could I be mad? I mean, it was Douglas. It would be like being mad at the wind. The wind can't help blowing. Douglas can't help being a complete and utter moron sometimes.

Well, not just Douglas, either. A lot of boys can't, I've noticed.

"Great," I said with a sigh.

"I'm really sorry, Jess," Douglas said.

He really sounded it, too.

"Oh, don't worry about it," I said. "I'm not so sure I'm cut out for this camp counselor stuff anyway."

Now sounding surprised, Douglas said, "Jess, I can't think of a job more perfect for you."

I was shocked to hear this. "Really?"

"Really. I mean, you don't—what's the word?—condescend to kids like a lot of people do. You treat them like you treat everybody else. You know. Shitty."

"Gee," I said. "Thanks."

"You're welcome," Douglas said. "Oh, and Dad says anytime you want to quit and come on back home, the steam table's waiting for you."

"Ha-ha," I said. "How's Mikey?"

"Mike? He's trying to get as many glimpses of Claire Lippman in her underwear as he can before he leaves for Harvard at the end of August."

"It's good to have a hobby," I said.

"And Mom's making you a dress." You could tell Douglas was totally enjoying himself, now that he'd gotten over giving me the bad news. "She's got this idea that you're going to be nominated for homecoming queen this year, so you'd better have a dress for the occasion."

Of course. Because thirty years ago, my mom had been nominated homecoming queen of the very same high school I was currently going to. Why shouldn't I follow in her footsteps?

Um, how about because I am a mutated freak? But my mom stubbornly refuses to believe this. We mostly just let her live in her fantasy world, since it's easier than trying to drag her into the real one.

"And that's about it," Douglas said. "Got any messages for anybody? Want me to tell Rosemary anything?"

"*Douglas,*" I hissed in a warning tone.

"Oops," he said. "Sorry."

"I better go," I said. I could hear someone coming down the hall. "Thanks for the heads up and all. I guess."

"Well," Douglas said. "I just thought you should know. About the guy, I mean. In case he shows up, or whatever."

Great. Just what I needed. Some reporter showing up at Lake Wawasee to interview Lightning Girl. Pamela wouldn't freak too much about that.

"Okay," I said. "Well, bye, Catbreath." I used my pet name for Douglas from when we were small.

He returned the favor. "See ya, Buttface."

I hung up. Down the hall, I heard keys rattle. Pamela was just locking up her office. She came out into the main reception area.

"Everything all right at home?" she asked me, sounding as if she actually cared.

I thought about the question. *Was* everything all right at home? Had everything *ever* been all right at home? No. Of course not.

And I didn't think it'd be too much of a stretch to say that everything would never be all right at home.

But that's not what I told Pamela.

"Sure," I said, hugging the padded envelope to my chest. "Everything's great."

CHAPTER

4

I was forced to eat those words a second later, however, when I stepped outside the camp's administrative offices, into the sticky twilight, and heard it.

Someone screaming. Someone screaming my name.

Pamela heard it, too. She looked at me curiously. I didn't have time for questions, though. I took off running in the direction the screams were coming from. Pamela followed me. I could hear her office keys and loose change jangling in the pockets of her khaki shorts.

Dinner was over. The kids were streaming out of the dining hall and heading over toward the Pit for their first campfire. I saw kids of all sizes and colors, but the two to whom my gaze was instantly drawn were, of course, Shane and Lionel. This time, Shane had Lionel in a headlock. He wasn't choking him, or anything. He just wouldn't let go.

"It's okay, Lionel," Shane was saying. He pronounced it the American way, LIE-oh-nell. "They're just dogs. They're not going to hurt you."

The camp dogs, barking and wagging their tails delightedly, were leaping around, trying to lick Lionel and just about any other kid they could catch. Lionel, being so short, was getting most of these licks in the face.

"See, I know in Gonorrhea, you eat dogs," Shane was saying, "but here in America, see, we keep dogs as pets. . . ."

"Jess!" Lionel screamed. His thin voice broke with a sob. "Jess!"

There was a group of kids gathered around, watching Shane torture the smaller boy. Have you ever noticed how this always happens? I have. I mean, I know whenever I take a swing at somebody, people immediately come flocking to the area, eager to watch the fight. No one ever tries to break it up. No one ever goes, "Hey, Jess, why don't you just let the guy go?" No way. It's like why people go to car races: They want to see someone crash.

I waded through the kids and dogs until I reached Shane. I couldn't do what I wanted to, since I knew Pamela was right behind me. Instead, I said, "Shane, let him go."

Shane looked up at me, his eyes—which were already small—going even smaller.

"Whadduya mean?" he demanded. "I'm just showing him how the dogs aren't gonna hurt him.

See, he's afraid of them. I'm doing him a favor. I'm trying to help him overcome his phobia—"

Lionel, by this time, was openly sobbing. The dogs licked away his tears before they had a chance to trickle down his face very far.

I could hear Pamela's keys still jangling behind me. She wasn't, I realized, on the scene quite yet. Clutching my envelope in one hand, I reached out with the other and, placing my thumb and middle finger just above Shane's elbow, squeezed as hard as I could.

Shane let out a shriek and let go of Lionel just as Pamela broke through the crowd that had gathered around us.

"What—" she demanded, bewilderedly, "is going on here?"

Lionel, free at last, hurled himself at me, flinging his arms around my waist and burying his face in my stomach so the dogs couldn't get at his tears.

"They try to kill me!" he was screaming. "Jess, Jess, those dogs are try to kill me."

Shane, meanwhile, was massaging his funny bone. "Whaddidja have to go and do that for?" he demanded. "You know, if it turns out I can't play anymore on account of you, my dad's going to sue you—"

"Shane." I put one hand on Lionel's shaking shoulders and, with the envelope, pointed toward the Pit. "You've got one strike. Now go."

"A strike?" Shane looked up at me incredulously. "A *strike*? What's a *strike*? What'd I get a *strike* for?"

"You know what you got it for," I said, answering his last question first. The truth was, I hadn't figured out the answer to his first question. But one thing I did know: "Two more, and you're out, buddy. Now go sit with the others at the campfire and keep your hands to yourself."

Shane stamped a sneakered foot. "Out? You can't do that. You can't throw me out."

"Watch me."

Shane turned his accusing stare toward Pamela. Unlike when he was looking at me, he actually had to tilt his chin a little to see her eyes.

"Can she do that?" he demanded.

Pamela, to my relief, said, "Of course she can. Now all of you, go to the Pit."

Nobody moved. Pamela said, "I said, *go*."

Something in her voice made them do what she said. Now *that's* an ability I wouldn't mind having: making people do what I told them, without having to resort to doing them bodily harm.

Lionel continued to cling to me, still sobbing. The dogs had not gone away. In the usual manner of animals, they had realized that Lionel wanted nothing to do with them, and so they remained stubbornly at his side, looking at him with great interest, their tongues ready and waiting for him to turn around so they could continue lapping up his tears.

"Lionel," I said, giving the little boy's shoulder a shake. "The dogs really won't hurt you. They're good dogs. I mean, if any of them had ever hurt anyone, do you think they would be allowed to stay? No way. It would open the camp up to all sorts of law-suits. You know how litigious the parents of gifted children can be." Shane being example numero uno.

Pamela raised her eyebrows at this but said noth-ing, letting me handle the situation in my own way. Eventually, Lionel took his head out of my midriff and blinked up at me tearfully. The dogs, though they stirred eagerly at this motion, stayed where they were.

"I don't know what this means, this 'litigious,' " Lionel said. "But I thank you for helping me, Jess."

I reached out and patted his springy hair. "Don't mention it. Now, watch."

I stuck my hand out. The dogs, recognizing some sort of weird human/dog signal, rushed forward and began licking my fingers.

"See?" I said as Lionel watched, wide-eyed. "They're just interested in making friends." Or in the smell of all the Fiddle Faddle I'd handled earlier, but whatever.

"I see." Lionel regarded the dogs with wide dark eyes. "I will not be afraid, then. But . . . is it permissi-ble for me not to touch them?"

"Sure," I said. I withdrew my hand, which felt as if I'd just dipped it into a vat of hot mayonnaise. I wiped it off on my shorts. "Why don't you go join the rest of the Birch Trees?"

Lionel gave me a tremulous smile, then hurried toward the Pit, with many furtive glances over his shoulder at the dogs. I don't think he noticed that Pamela and I had as many by the collar as we could hold.

"Well," Pamela said when Lionel was out of earshot. "You certainly handled that . . . interestingly."

"That Shane," I said. "He's a pill."

"He is a challenge," Pamela corrected me. "He does seem to get worse every year."

I shook my head. "Tell me about it." I was beginning to wonder if Andrew, whose cabin I'd inherited, had heard through the grapevine that Shane had been assigned to it, and then lied about having mono to get out of having to spend his summer dealing with that particular "challenge." Andrew was a "returner." He'd worked at the camp the summer before as well.

"Why do you let him come back?" I asked.

Pamela sighed. "I realize you wouldn't know it to look at him, but Shane's actually extremely gifted."

"*Shane* is?"

My astonishment must have shown in my voice, since Pamela nodded vigorously as she said, "Oh, yes, it's true. The boy is a musical genius. Perfect pitch, you know."

I just shook my head. "Get out of town."

"I'm serious. Not to mention the fact that . . . well, his parents are very . . . generous with their support."

Well. That pretty much said it all, didn't it?

I joined my fellow Birch Trees—and the rest of the camp—around the fire. The first night's campfire was devoted almost entirely to staff introductions and acquainting the campers with Camp Wawasee's many rules. All of the musical instructors were paraded out, along with the rest of the camp staff—the counselors, the administrators, the lifeguards, the handymen, the nurse, the cafeteria workers, and so on.

Then we went over the list of rules and regulations: no running; no littering; no one allowed out of the cottages after 10:00 P.M.; no cabin raids; no diving into the lake; no playing of musical instruments outside of the practice rooms (this was a crucial rule, because if everyone tried to practice outside of the soundproof rooms provided for that purpose, the camp would soon sound worse than a traffic jam at rush hour). We learned about how Camp Wawasee was smack in the middle of five hundred acres of federally protected forest, and how, if any one of us went wandering off into this forest, we should pretty much expect never to be heard from again.

On this encouraging note, we were reminded that the mandatory Polar Bear swim commenced at seven in the morning. Then, after a few rounds of *Dona Nobis Pacem* (hey, it was orchestra camp, after all), we were dismissed for the night.

Shane was at my side the minute I stood up.

"Hey," he said, tugging on my shirt. "What happens if I get three strikes?"

"You're out," I informed him.

"But you can't throw me out of the camp." Shane's freckles—he had quite a lot of them—stood out in the firelight. "You try to do that, my dad'll sue you."

See what I meant, about gifted kids' parents being litigious?

"I'm not going to throw you out of camp," I said. "But I might throw you out of the cabin."

Shane glared at me. "Whadduya mean?"

"Make you sleep on the porch," I said. "Without benefit of air-conditioning."

Shane laughed. He actually laughed and went, "That's my punishment? Sleep without air-conditioning?"

He cackled all the way back to the cottage, and accrued another strike when, along the way, he threw a rock—supposedly at a firefly, or so he claimed—which just happened to miss Lionel by only about an inch and ended up hitting Arthur—who took out his feelings on the matter with prompt assertiveness. I, relieved to see that at least one member of Birch Tree Cottage could defend himself against Shane, did nothing to stop the fight.

"Jeez," Scott said. He and Dave, their own campers having obediently gone on ahead to their cabins—and probably brushed their teeth and tucked themselves in already—paused beside me to observe Shane and Arthur's wrestling match, which was happening off the lighted path, and in what appeared to be a dense patch of poison ivy. "What'd you ever do to deserve *that* kid?"

Watching the fight, I shrugged. "Born under an unlucky star, I guess."

"That kid," Dave said, watching as Shane tried, unsuccessfully, to grind Arthur's face into some tree roots, "is just destined to take an Uzi to his home-room teacher someday."

"Maybe I should stop this—" Scott started to step off the path.

I grabbed his arm. "Oh, no," I said. "Let's let them get it out of their systems." Arthur had just gotten the upper hand, and was seated on Shane's chest.

"Say you're sorry," Arthur commanded Shane, "or I'll bounce up and down until your ribs break."

Scott and Dave and I, impressed by this threat, looked at one another with raised eyebrows.

"Jess!" Shane wailed.

"Shane," I said, "if you're going to throw rocks, you have to be prepared to pay the consequences."

"But he's going to kill me!"

"Just like you could have killed him with that rock."

"He wouldn't have died from that rock," Shane howled. "It was a little itty-bitty rock."

"It could have put his eye out," I said in my prissi-est voice. Scott and Dave both had to turn away, lest the boys catch them laughing.

"When you break a rib," Arthur informed his quarry, "you can't breathe from your diaphragm. You know, when you play. Because it hurts so much. Don't know how you're going to sustain those whole notes when—"

"GET OFFA ME!" Shane roared.

Arthur scooped up a handful of dirt, apparently with the intention of shoveling it into Shane's mouth.

"All right, all right," Shane bellowed. "I'm sorry."

Arthur let him up. Shane, following him back to the path, gave me a dirty look and said, "Wait until my dad finds out what a sucky counselor you are. He'll get you fired for sure."

"Gosh," I said. "You mean I might have to leave here and never listen to your whining voice again? What a punishment."

Furious, Shane stormed off toward Birch Tree Cottage. Arthur, chuckling, followed him.

"Jeez," Scott said again. "You want help putting those guys to bed?"

I knit my brow. "What are you talking about? They're almost twelve years old. They don't need to be put to bed."

He just shook his head.

About half an hour later, I realized what he'd been talking about. It was close to ten, but none of the residents of Birch Tree Cottage were in bed. None of them were even in their pajamas. In fact, they were doing everything *but* getting ready for bed. Some of them were jumping on the beds. Others were racing around the beds. A few had climbed under their beds, into the cubbies where they were supposed to stash their clothes.

But none of them were actually in the beds.

Somehow, I couldn't see any of this happening in Frangipani Cottage. Karen Sue Hanky, I was willing to bet, was probably braiding somebody's hair right now, while somebody else told ghost stories and they all enjoyed a big bowl of buttered popcorn from the utility kitchen.

Popcorn. My stomach rumbled at the thought. I hadn't had any dinner. I was starving. I was starving, Birch Tree Cottage was out of control, and I still hadn't had a chance to open that envelope Pamela had given to me to give to Ruth.

Except, of course, that what was inside the envelope was really for me.

It was the idea of the ghost stories that did it, I guess. I couldn't shriek over the screaming, and I couldn't catch any of the kids who were racing around, but I could make it a lot harder for them to see. I stalked over to the fuse box and, one by one, threw the switches.

The cottage was plunged into blackness. It's amazing how dark things can get out in the country. They had switched off the lights along the paths through camp, since everyone was supposed to be in bed, so there wasn't even any light from outdoors to creep in through the windows—especially since the area we were in was so thickly wooded, not even moonbeams could penetrate the canopy of leaves overhead. I couldn't see my own hand in front of my face.

And the other residents of Birch Tree Cottage were suffering from a similar difficulty. I heard several thumps as the runners collided with pieces of furniture, and a number of people shrieked as the lights went out.

Then frightened voices began to call out my name.

"Oops," I said. "Power outage. There must be a storm somewhere."

More frightened whimpering.

"I guess," I said, "we'll all just have to go to sleep. Because we can't do anything in the dark."

It was Shane's voice that rang out scathingly, "There's no power outage. You turned out the lights."

Little brat.

"I didn't," I said. "Come over here, and try the switch." I illustrated for them, flicking the switch on and off. The sound was unmistakable. "I guess everybody better get into their pajamas and get into bed."

There was a good deal of moaning and groaning about how were they supposed to find their pajamas in the dark. There was also some bickering about the fact that they couldn't brush their teeth in the dark, and what if they got cavities, et cetera. I ignored it. I had found, in the utility kitchen, a flashlight, for use in the event of a real blackout, and I offered to escort whoever wanted to go to the bathroom.

Shane said, "Just give me the flashlight, and I'll escort everyone," but I wasn't falling for that one.

After everyone had done what he needed to do, ablution-wise, I reminded them all about the early morning Polar Bear swim, and that they had better get plenty of sleep, since their first music lessons would begin right after breakfast. The only time they wouldn't be playing their instruments, in fact, would be at the Polar Bear swim, meals, and a two-hour period from three to five, when lake swims, tennis, baseball, and arts and crafts were allowed. There were nature walks, for those who were so inclined. There even used to be trips to Wolf Cave, a semi-famous cave near the lake—semi-famous because up so far north, caves are almost unheard of, the glaciers having flattened most of upstate Indiana. But of course some stupid camper had gotten himself whacked on the head by a falling stalactite, or something, so now spelunking was no longer listed as one of the activities allowed during the kids' few short hours of free time.

It seemed to me that for kids, the campers at Lake Wawasee weren't allowed a whole lot of time to be . . . well, just kids.

When they were all in their beds, and had sweetly sang out good night to me, I took the flashlight with me into my own room. No sense adjusting the fuse box so that my own light would turn on: they'd just see it, shining out from under the crack in the door, and know I'd lied to them about the power outage. I took off my counselor shirt and shorts, and, in a pair of boxers I'd stolen from Douglas and a tank top, I consumed most of a box of Fiddle Faddle while perusing, by flashlight beam, the contents of the envelope Pamela had given me to give to Ruth.

Dear Jess,
I hope this finds you well. Your camp counselor job sounds like a lot of fun.

Yeah, right, I grunted to myself. Of course it sounded like fun . . . to people who'd never had the displeasure of meeting Shane, anyway. The very feminine cursive went on.

Enclosed please find a photo of Taylor Monroe.

I shined the beam from the flashlight into the envelope and found a color studio portrait—like the kind you would get at Sears, with Sesame Street in the background—of a curly-headed toddler in overalls. OshKosh B'gosh.

Taylor disappeared from a shopping mall two years ago, when he was three years old. His parents are desperate to get him back. The police have no suspects or leads.

Good. A neat and simple kidnapping. Rosemary had done a lot of homework to make sure of this. She only sent me the cases in which she was certain the kid in question actually wanted to be found. It was my only condition for finding the kids: that they really wanted to be found.

Well, that, and maintaining my anonymity, of course.

As always, call if you find him. You know the number.

The letter was signed, *Love, Rosemary.*

I studied the photo in the beam from my flashlight. Taylor Monroe, I said to myself. Taylor Monroe, where are you?

The door to my room banged open, and I dropped the photo—and the flashlight—in my surprise.

"Hey," Shane said with interest. "What's that stuff?"

"Jeez," I said, scrambling to hide the photo and letter in my sheets. "Ever heard of knocking?"

"Who's the kid?" Shane wanted to know.

"None of your business." I found the flashlight and shined it on him. "What do you want?"

Shane's eyes narrowed, but not just because there was a bright light shining into them. They narrowed with suspicion.

"Hey," he said. "That's a picture of a missing kid, isn't it?"

Well, Pamela had been right about one thing, anyway. Shane was gifted. And not just musically, either, it appeared. The kid was sharp.

"Don't be ridiculous," I said.

"Oh, yeah? Well, what are you hiding it for, then?"

"Shane." I couldn't believe this. "What do you want?"

Shane ignored my question, however.

"You lied," he said, sounding indignant. "You totally lied. You *do* still have those powers."

"Yeah, that's right, Shane," I said. "That's why I'm working here at Camp Wawasee for five bucks an hour. I have psychic powers and all, and could be raking in the bucks finding missing people for the government, but I prefer to hang around here."

Shane's only response to my sarcasm was to blink a few times.

"Come off it," I said sourly. "Okay? Now why are you out of bed?"

The look of dark suspicion didn't leave Shane's face, but he did manage to remember his fake excuse for barging in on me, undoubtedly in an effort to catch me sans apparel. He whined, "I want a drink of water."

"So go get one," I said, not very nicely.

"I can't see my way to the bathroom," he whined some more.

"You found your way here," I pointed out to him.

"But—"

"Get out, Shane."

He left, still whining. I fished out Taylor's photo and Rosemary's letter. I didn't feel bad about lying to Shane. Not at all. I'd done it as much to protect Rosemary as myself. After my run-in last spring with the U.S. government, whose ideas about the best way to use my psychic ability had sort of differed from mine, Rosemary, a receptionist who worked at a foundation that helped find missing children, had very generously agreed to help me . . . um, well, privatize. And we had been working together, undiscovered, ever since.

And I wanted things to stay that way between us: undiscovered. I would not risk revealing our secret even to a whiny almost-twelve-year-old musical genius like Shane.

To be on the safe side, I put away Rosemary's letter and picked up a copy of *Cosmo* Ruth had lent me. "10 Ways to Tell He Thinks of You as More Than Just a Friend." Ooh. Good stuff. I read eagerly, wondering if I'd realize, just from reading this article, that Rob really did like me, only I had simply been too stupid to read the signs.

1. He cooks you dinner on your birthday.

Well, Rob certainly hadn't done that. But my birthday was in April. He and I hadn't really started . . . well, whatever it was we were doing . . . until May. So that one was no good.

2. He makes an attempt to get along with your girl-friends.

I only have one real friend, and that's Ruth. She's barely even met Rob. Well, not really. See, Rob's from what you might call the wrong side of the tracks. Ruth isn't a snob . . . at least, not really . . . but she definitely wouldn't approve of me going out with someone who didn't have college and a career as a professional in his sights.

So much for Number 2.

3. He listens to you when—

I was interrupted by a thump. It was followed immediately by a wail.

Gripping my flashlight, I stalked out of my room.

"All right," I said, shining the flashlight into one face after another—all of which were very much awake. "What gives?"

When the light from my flashlight reached Lionel's face, it picked up the tear tracks down his cheeks.

"Why are you crying?" I demanded. But I knew. That thump I heard. Shane was in his bed, some feet away, but his face looked too sweetly innocent for him to not be guilty of something.

But all Lionel would say was, "I am not crying."

I was sick of it. I really was. All I wanted to do was read my magazine and go to bed, so I could find Taylor Monroe. Was that so much to ask, after such a long day?

"Fine," I said, sitting down on the floor, my flashlight shining against the ceiling.

Arthur went, "Uh, Jess? What are you doing?"

"I am going to sit here," I said, "until you all fall asleep."

This caused some excited giggling. Don't ask me why.

There was silence for maybe ten seconds. Then Doo Sun went, "Jess? Do you have any brothers?"

Guardedly, I replied in the affirmative.

"I thought so," Doo Sun said.

Instantly suspicious, I asked, "Why?"

"You're wearing boys' underpants," Paul pointed out.

I looked down. I'd forgotten about Douglas's boxers.

"So I am," I said.

"Jess," Shane said, in a voice so sugary, I knew he was up to no good.

"What," I said flatly.

"Are you a lesbian?"

I closed my eyes. I counted to ten. I tried to ignore the giggling from the other beds.

I opened my eyes and said, "No, I am not a lesbian. As a matter of fact, I have a boyfriend."

"Who?" Arthur wanted to know. "One of those guys I saw you with on the path? One of those other counselors?"

This caused a certain amount of suggestive hooting. I said, "No. My boyfriend would never do anything as geeky as be a camp counselor. My boyfriend rides a Harley and is a car mechanic."

This caused some appreciative murmuring. Eleven-year-old boys are much more impressed by car mechanics than people like . . . well, my best friend, Ruth, for instance.

Then . . . don't ask me why—maybe I was still thinking about Karen Sue over there in Frangipani Cottage. But suddenly, I launched into this story about Rob, and about how once this guy had brought a car into Wilkins's Auto that turned out to have a skeleton in the trunk.

It was, of course, a complete fabrication. As I went on about Rob and this car, which turned out to be haunted, on account of the woman who'd been left to suffocate in its trunk, I borrowed liberally from Stephen King, incorporating aspects from both

Maximum Overdrive and *Christine*. These kids were too young, of course, to have read the books, and I doubted their parents had ever let them see the movies.

And I was right. I held them enthralled all the way until the fiery cataclysm at the end, in which Rob saved our entire town by bravely pointing a grenade launcher at the renegade automobile and blowing it into a thousand pieces.

Stunned silence followed this pronouncement. I had, I could tell, greatly disturbed them. But I was not done.

"And sometimes," I whispered, "on nights like this, when a storm somewhere far away douses the power, blanketing us in darkness, you can still see the headlights of that killer car, way off on the horizon"—I flicked off the flashlight—"way off in the distance . . . coming closer . . . and closer . . . and closer . . ."

Not a sound. They were hardly breathing.

"Good night," I said, and went back into my room.

Where I fell asleep a few minutes later, after finishing the box of Fiddle Faddle.

And I didn't hear another peep out of my fellow residents of Birch Tree Cottage until after reveille the next morning. . . .

By which time, of course, I knew precisely where Taylor Monroe was.

CHAPTER

5

"I was so scared, I almost wet the bed," said John.

"Yeah? Well, I was so scared, I couldn't get out of bed, not even to go to the bathroom." Sam had a towel slung around his neck. His chest was so thin, it was practically concave. "I just held it," he said. "I didn't want to run the risk, you know, of seeing those headlights out the window."

"I saw them," Tony declared.

There were general noises of derision at this.

"No, really," Tony said. "Through the window. I swear. It looked like they were floating over the lake."

A heated discussion followed about whether or not Rob's killer car could float, or if it had merely hovered over the lake.

Standing in line for the Polar Bear swim, I began to feel that things were not nearly so bleak as they'd seemed yesterday. For one thing, I'd had a good night's sleep.

Really. I know that sounds surprising, considering that while I'd slept, my brain waves had apparently been bombarded with all this information about a five-year-old kid I had never met. On TV and in books and stuff, psychics always get this tortured look on their faces when they get a vision, like someone is jabbing them with a toothpick, or whatever. But that's never happened to me. Maybe it's because I only get my psychic visions while I sleep, but none of them have ever hurt.

The way I see it, it's exactly like all those times you've been sitting there thinking to yourself, Gee, So-and-So hasn't called in a while, and all of a sudden the phone rings, and it's So-and-So. And you're all, "Dude, I was just thinking about you," and you laugh because it's a big coincidence.

Only it's not. It's not a coincidence. That was the psychic part of your brain working, the part hardly any of us ever listens to, the part people call "intuition" or "gut feeling" or "instinct." That's the part of my brain that the lightning, when it struck me, sent all haywire. And that's why I'm a receiver now for all sorts of information I shouldn't have—like the fact that Taylor Monroe, who'd disappeared from a shopping center in Des Moines two years ago, was now living in Gainesville, Florida, with some people to whom he wasn't even remotely related.

See, ordinary people—most everyone, really, even

smart people, like Einstein and Madonna—use only three percent of their brain. Three percent! That's all it takes to learn to walk and talk and make change and parallel park and decide which flavor of yogurt is your favorite.

But some people—people like me, who've been hit by lightning, or put into a sensory deprivation tank, or whatever—use more than their three percent. For whatever reason, we've tapped into the other ninety-seven percent of our brain.

And that's the part, apparently, where all the good stuff is. . . .

Except that the only stuff I seem to have access to is the current address of just about every missing person in the universe.

Well, it was better than nothing, I guess.

But yeah, okay? In spite of the psychic vision thing, I'd slept great.

I don't think the same could be said for my fellow campers—and their counselors. Ruth in particular looked bleary-eyed.

"My God," she said. "They kept me up all night. They just kept yakking. . . ." Her blue eyes widened behind her glasses as she got a better look at me. I was in my bathing suit, just like my boys, with a towel slung around my own neck. "God, you're not actually going *in*, are you?"

I shrugged. "Sure." What else was I supposed to do? I was going to have to call Rosemary, as soon as I could get my hands on a phone. But that, I was pretty sure, wasn't going to be for hours.

"You don't have to," Ruth said. "I mean, it's just for the kids. . . ."

"Well, it's not like I could take a shower this morning," I reminded her. "Not with eight budding little sex maniacs around."

Ruth looked from me to the bright blue water, sparkling in the morning sun. "Suit yourself," she said. "But you're going to smell like chlorine all day."

"Yeah," I said. "And who's going to get close enough to smell me?"

We both looked over at Todd. He, too, was in a bathing suit. And looking very impressive in it, as well, I might add.

"Not him," I said.

Ruth sighed. "No, I guess not."

I noticed that while Todd might be ignoring us, Scott and Dave definitely weren't. They both looked away when I glanced in their direction, but there was no question about it: they'd been scoping.

Ruth, however, only had eyes for Todd.

"And you have your tutorial today," she was pointing out. "I thought that flute guy was pretty hot. You don't want to smell chlorine-y for *him*, do you?"

"That flute guy" was the wind instructor, a French dude name Jean-Paul something or other. He was kind of hot, in a scruffy-looking French kind of way. But he was a little old for me. I mean, I like my men older, and all, but I think thirty might be pushing it a little. How weird would *that* look at prom?

"I don't know," I said as our line moved closer to the water. "He's Do-able, I guess. But no Hottie."

I hadn't realized Karen Sue Hanky was eavesdropping until she spun around and, with flashing but deeply circled eyes, snarled, "I hope you aren't speaking of Professor Le Blanc. He happens to be a musical genius, you know."

I rolled my eyes. "Who *isn't* a musical genius around here?" I wanted to know. "Except you, of course, Karen."

Ruth, who'd been chewing gum, swallowed it in her effort not to laugh.

"I resent that," Karen said, slowly turning as red as the letters on the lifeguard's T-shirt. "I will have you know that I have been practicing for four hours a day, and that my dad's paying thirty dollars an hour to a professor who's been giving me private lessons over at the university."

"Yeah?" I raised my eyebrows. "Gosh, maybe you'll be able to keep up with the rest of us now."

Karen narrowed her eyes at me.

But whatever she'd been going to say was drowned out when the lifeguard—who was also pretty cute: definitely Do-able—blew a whistle and yelled, "Birch Tree!"

My fellow birches and I made a run for the water and jumped in simultaneously, with much shrieking and splashing. Some of us were better swimmers than others, and there was much choking and sputtering, and at least one attempted drowning, which the lifeguard spotted. Shane was forced to sit out for twenty minutes. But, otherwise, we had a good time.

I was teaching them a new song—since Pamela had put the kibosh on "I Met a Miss"—when Scott and Dave and Ruth and Karen strolled by with their campers. All of them, I noticed, looked a little bleary around the edges.

"I don't understand how you can be so wide awake," Scott said. "Didn't they keep you up all night?"

"No," I said. "Not at all."

"What's your secret?" Dave wanted to know. "Mine were bouncing off the walls. I had to sleep with a pillow over my head."

Ruth shook her head. "Their first night away from home," she said knowingly. "It's always the toughest. They usually settle down by the third or fourth night, out of sheer exhaustion."

Karen Sue exhaled gustily. "Not mine, I'll bet." She glared at some passing Frangipanis, who giggled and tore off along the path, causing all of us to chime, in unison, *"Walk, don't run!"*

"They are little monsters," Karen muttered, under her breath. "Won't do a thing I say, and the mouths on them! I never heard such language in all my life! And all night long, it was giggle, giggle, giggle."

"Me, too," Ruth said tiredly. "They didn't nod off until around five, I think."

"Five-thirty for me," Scott said. He looked at me. "I can't believe that Shane of yours just slipped off to Slumberland without a fight."

"Yeah," Dave said. "What's your secret?"

I honestly didn't know any better. I said, cheerfully, "Oh, I just told them all this really long story, and they nodded off right away. We all slept like stones. Didn't wake up until reveille."

Ruth, astonished, said, "Really?"

"What was the story about?" Dave wanted to know.

Laughingly, I told them. Not about Rob, of course, but about the killer car, and the appropriating of some of Mr. King's works.

They listened in stunned silence. Then Karen said vehemently, "I don't believe in frightening children with ghost stories."

I snorted. Karen, of course, didn't know what she was talking about. What kid didn't love a ghost story? Ghost stories weren't the problem. But the fact that a three-year-old could be kidnapped from a mall and not be found until two years later?

Now *that* was scary.

Which was why, instead of joining my fellow Birch Trees for breakfast that morning—even though I was starving, of course, after my swim and my Fiddle Faddle dinner of the night before—I snuck back into the camp's administrative offices, in the hopes of finding a phone I could use.

I scored one without a lot of trouble. The secretary with the NASCAR-driving boyfriend wasn't in yet. I slipped into her chair and, dialing nine first to get out, dialed the number to the National Organization for Missing Children.

Rosemary didn't pick up. Some other lady did.

"1-800-WHERE-R-YOU," she said. "How may I direct your call?"

I had to whisper, of course, so I wouldn't be overheard. I also assumed my best Spanish accent, just in case the line was being monitored. "Rosemary, *por favor.*"

The lady went, "Excuse me?"

I whispered, "*Rosemary.*"

"Oh," the lady said. "Um. One moment."

Jeez! I didn't have a moment! I could be busted any *second.* All I needed was for Pamela to walk in and find that not only had I abandoned my charges, but I was also making personal use of camp property. . . .

"This is Rosemary," a voice said, cautiously, into my ear.

"Hey," I said, dropping the Spanish accent. There was no need to say who was calling. Rosemary knew my voice. "Taylor Monroe. Gainesville, Florida." I rattled off the street address. Because that's how it comes. The information, I mean. It's like there's a search engine inside of my brain: insert name and photo image of missing child, and out comes full address, often with zip code attached, of where child can be located.

Seriously. It's bizarre, especially considering I've never even heard of most of these places.

"Thank you," Rosemary said, careful not to say my name within hearing of her supervisor, who'd sicced the Feds on me once before. "They're going to be so happy. You don't know—"

It was at this point that Pamela, looking troubled, came striding down the hall, heading straight toward the secretary's desk.

I whispered, "Sorry, Rosemary, gotta go," and hung up the phone. Then I ducked beneath the desk.

It didn't do any good, though. I was busted. Way busted.

Pamela went, "Jess?"

I curled into a tight ball underneath the secretary's desk. Maybe, if I didn't move, didn't even breathe, Pamela would think she had seen a mirage or something, and go away.

"Jessica," Pamela said, in the kind of voice you probably wouldn't use if you were talking to a mirage. "Come out. I saw you."

Sheepishly, I crawled out from beneath the desk.

"Look," I said. "I can explain. It's my grandma's ninetieth birthday today, and if I didn't call first thing, well, there'd be H to pay—"

I thought I'd get brownie points for saying H instead of hell, but it didn't work out that way. For one thing, Pamela had looked as if she'd already been in a bad mood before she saw me. Now she was even more upset.

"Jess," she said in a weird voice. "You know you aren't supposed to be using camp property—"

"—for personal calls," I finished for her. "Yes, I know. And I'm really sorry. Like I said, it was an emergency."

Pamela looked way more upset than the situation warranted. I knew something else was up. But I figured it was some kind of orchestra camp emergency or something. You know, like they'd run out of clarinet reeds.

But of course that wasn't it. Of course it turned out to have something to do with me after all.

"Jess," Pamela said. "I was just going to look for you."

"You were?" I blinked at her. There was only one reason for Pamela to have been looking for me, and that was that I was in trouble. Again.

And the only thing I'd done recently—besides make a personal call from a camp phone—was the whole ghost story thing. Had Karen Sue ratted me out for that? If so, it had to be a record. I had left her barely five minutes ago. What did the girl have, bionic feet?

It was clear that Pamela was on Karen Sue's side about the whole not frightening little children thing. I could see I was going to have to do some fast talking.

"Look," I said. "I can explain. Shane was completely out of control last night, and the only way I could get him to stop picking on the littler kids was to—"

"Jessica," Pamela interrupted, sort of sharply. "I don't know what you're talking about. There's . . . there's actually someone here to see you."

I shut up and just stared at her. "Someone here?" I echoed lamely. "To see *me?*"

A thousand things went through my head. The first thing I thought was . . . Douglas. Douglas's phone call the night before. He hadn't just been calling to say he missed me. He'd been calling to say good-bye. He'd finally done it. The voices had told him to, and so he had. Douglas had killed himself, and my dad—my mother—my other brother—one of them was here to break the news to me.

A roaring sound started in my ears. I felt as if the bottom had dropped out of my stomach.

"Where?" I asked, through lips that felt like they were made of ice.

Pamela nodded, her expression grave, toward her office door. I moved toward it slowly, with Pamela following close behind. Let it be Michael, I prayed. Let them have sent Mikey to break the news to me. Michael I could take. If it was my mother, or even my father, I was bound to start crying. And I didn't want to cry in front of Pamela.

It wasn't Mikey, though. It wasn't my father, either, or even my mother. It was a man I'd never seen before.

He was older than me, but younger than my parents. He looked to be about Pamela's age. Still, he was definitely Do-able. He may have even qualified for Hottie. Clean-shaven, with dark, slightly longish hair, he had on a tie and sports coat. When my gaze fell upon him, he climbed hastily to his feet, and I saw that he was quite tall—well, everyone is, to me—and not very graceful.

"M-Miss Mastriani?" he asked in a shy voice.

Social worker? I wondered, taking in the fact that his shoes were well-worn, and the cuffs of his sports coat a bit frayed. Definitely not a Fed. He was too good-looking to be a Fed. He'd have drawn too much attention.

Schoolteacher, maybe. Yeah. Math or science. But why on earth would a math or science teacher be here to break the news about my brother Douglas's suicide?

"I'm Jonathan Herzberg," the man said, thrusting his right hand toward me. "I really hope you won't resent the intrusion. I understand that it is highly unusual, and a gross infringement on your rights to personal privacy and all of that . . . but the fact is, Miss Mastriani, I'm desperate." His brown-eyed gaze bore into mine. "Really, really desperate."

I took a step backward, away from the hand. I moved back so fast, I ended up with my butt against the edge of Pamela's desk.

A reporter. I should have known. The tie should have been a dead giveaway.

"Look," I said.

The icy feeling had left my lips. The roaring in my ears had stopped. The feeling that the bottom of my stomach had dropped out? Yeah, that had disappeared. Instead, I just felt anger.

Cold, hard anger.

"I don't know what paper you're from," I said stonily. "Or magazine or news show or whatever. But I have had just about enough of you guys. You all practically ruined my life this past spring, following me around, bugging my family. Well, it's over, okay?

Get it through your heads: lightning girl has hung up her bolts. I am not in the missing person business anymore."

Jonathan Herzberg looked more than a little taken aback. He glanced from me to Pamela and then back again.

"M-Miss Mastriani," he stammered. "I'm not . . . I mean, I don't—"

"Mr. Herzberg isn't a reporter, Jess." Pamela's voice was, for her, uncharacteristically soft. That, more than anything, got my attention. "We never allow reporters—and we have had our share of illustrious guests in the past—onto our property. Surely you know that."

I suppose I did know that, somewhere deep in the recesses of my mind. Lake Wawasee was private property. You had to be on a list of invited guests even to be let through the gates. They took security very seriously at Camp Wawasee, due to the number of expensive instruments lying around. Oh, and the kids, and all.

I looked from Pamela to Mr. Herzberg and then back again. They both looked . . . well, flushed. There was no other way to put it.

"Do you two know each other or something?" I asked.

Pamela, who was by no means what you'd call a shrinking violet kind of gal, actually blushed.

"No, no," she said. "I mean . . . well, we just met. Mr. Herzberg . . . well, Jess, Mr. Herzberg—"

I could see I was going to get nothing rational out of Miss J Crew. I decided to tackle Mr. L.L. Bean, instead.

"All right," I said, eyeing him. "I'll bite. If you're not a reporter, what do you want with me?"

Jonathan Herzberg wiped his hands on his khaki pants. He must have been sweating a lot or something, since he left damp spots on the cotton.

"I was hoping," he said softly, "that you could help me find my little girl."

CHAPTER

6

I looked quickly at Pamela. She hadn't taken her eyes off Jonathan Herzberg.

Great. Just great. Mary Ann was in love with the Professor.

"Maybe you didn't hear me the first time," I said. "I don't do that anymore."

A lie, of course. But he didn't know that.

Or maybe he did.

Mr. Herzberg said, "I know that's what you told everyone. Last spring, I mean. But I . . . well, I was hoping you only said that because the press and everything . . . well, it got a little intense."

I just looked at him. *Intense?* He called being chased by government goons with guns *intense?*

I'd show him intense.

"Hello?" I said. "What part of 'I can't help you' don't you understand? It doesn't work anymore. The psychic thing is played out. The batteries have run dry—"

As I'd been speaking, Mr. Herzberg had been digging around in his briefcase. When he stood up again, he was holding a photograph.

"This is her," he said, thrusting the photo into my hands. "This is Keely. She's only five—"

I backed away with about as much horror as if he'd put a snake, and not a photo of a little girl, into my fingers.

"I'm not looking at this," I said, practically heaving the photo back at him. "I *won't* look at this."

"Jess!" Pamela sounded a little horrified herself. "Jess, please, just listen—"

"No," I said. "No, I won't. You can't do this. I'm out of here."

Look, I know how it sounds. I mean, here was this guy, and he seemed sincere. He seemed like a genuinely distraught father. How could I be so cold, so unfeeling, not to want to help him?

Try looking at it from my point of view: It is one thing to get a package in the mail with all the details of a missing child's case laid neatly out in front of one . . . to wake the next morning and make a single phone call, the origins of which the person on the receiving end of that call has promised to erase. Easy.

More than just easy, though: Anonymous.

But it is another thing entirely to have the missing kid's parent in front of one, desperately begging for help. There is nothing easy about that.

And nothing in the least anonymous.

And I have to maintain my anonymity. I have to.

I turned and headed for the door. I was going to say, I staggered blindly for the door, because that sounds all dramatic and stuff, but it isn't true, exactly. I mean, I wasn't exactly staggering—I was walking just fine. And I could see and all. The way I know I could see just fine was that the photo, which I thought I'd gotten rid of, came fluttering down from the air where I'd thrown it. Just fluttered right down, and landed at my feet. Landed at my feet, right in front of the door, like a leaf or a feather or something that had fallen from the sky, and just randomly picked me to land in front of.

And I looked. It landed faceup. How could I help but look?

I'm not going to say anything dorky like she was the cutest kid I'd ever seen or something like that. That wasn't it. It was just that, until I saw the photo, she wasn't a real kid. Not to me. She was just something somebody was using to try to get me to admit something I didn't want to.

Then I saw her.

Look, I was not trying to be a bitch with this whole not-wanting-to-help-this-guy thing. Really. You just have to understand that since that day, that day I'd been struck by lightning, a lot of things had gotten very screwed up. I mean, really, really screwed up. My brother Douglas had had to be hospitalized again on account of me. I had practically ruined this other kid's life, just because I'd found him. *He hadn't wanted to be found.* I had had to do a lot of really tricky stuff to make everything right again.

And I'm not even going to go into the stuff about the Feds and the guns and the exploding helicopter and all.

It was like that day the lightning struck me, it caused this chain reaction that just kept getting more and more out of control, and all these people, all of these people I cared about, got hurt.

And I didn't want that to happen again. Not ever.

I had a pretty good system in the works, too, for seeing that it didn't. If everyone just played along the way they were supposed to, things went fine. Lost kids, kids who wanted to be found, got found. Nobody hassled me or my family. And things ran along pretty damn smoothly.

Then Jonathan Herzberg had to come along and thrust his daughter's photo under my nose.

And I knew. I knew it was happening all over again.

And there wasn't anything I could do to stop it.

Jonathan Herzberg was no dope. He saw the photo land. And he saw me look down.

And he went in for the kill.

"She's in kindergarten," he said. "Or at least, she would be starting in September, if . . . if she wasn't gone. She likes dogs and horses. She wants to be a veterinarian when she grows up. She's not afraid of anything."

I just stood there, looking down at the photo.

"Her mother has always been . . . troubled. After

Keely's birth, she got worse. I thought it was post-partum depression. Only it never went away. The doctors prescribed antidepressants. Sometimes she took them. Mostly, though, she didn't."

Jonathan Herzberg's voice was even and low. He wasn't crying or anything. It was like he was telling a story about someone else's wife, not his own.

"She started drinking. I came home from work one day, and she wasn't there. But Keely was. My wife had left a three-year-old child home, by herself, all day. She didn't come home until around midnight, and when she did, she was drunk. The next day, Keely and I moved out. I let her have the house, the car, everything . . . but not Keely." Now his voice started to sound a little shaky. "Since we left, she— my ex-wife—has just gotten worse. She's fallen in with this guy . . . well, he's not what you'd call a real savory character. And last week the two of them took Keely from the day care center I put her in. I think they're somewhere in the Chicago area—he has family around there—but the police haven't been able to find them. I just . . . I remembered about you, and I . . . I'm desperate. I called your house, and the person who answered the phone said—"

I bent down and picked the photo up. Up close, the kid looked no different than she had from the floor. She was a five-year-old little girl who wanted to be a veterinarian when she grew up, who lived with a father who obviously had as much of a clue as I did about how to braid hair, since Keely's was all over the place.

"He's got the custody papers," Pamela said to me softly. "I've seen them. When he first showed up . . . well, I didn't know what to do. You know our policy. But he . . . well, he . . ."

I knew what he had done. It was right there on Pamela's face. He had played on her natural affection for children, and on the fact that he was a single dad who was passably good-looking, and she was a woman in her thirties who wasn't married yet. It was as clear as the whistle around her neck.

I don't know what made me do it. Decide to help Jonathan Herzberg, I mean, in spite of my suspicion that he was an undercover agent, sent to prove I'd lied when I'd said I no longer had any psychic powers. Maybe it was the frayed condition of his cuffs. Maybe it was the messiness of his daughter's braids. In any case, I decided. I decided to risk it.

It was a decision that I'd live to regret, but how was I to know that then?

I guess what I did next must have startled them both, but to me, it was perfectly natural. Well, at least to someone who's seen *Point of No Return* as many times as I have.

I walked over to the radio I'd spied next to Pamela's desk, turned it on very loud, then yelled over the strains of John Mellencamp's latest, "Shirts up."

Pamela and Jonathan Herzberg exchanged wide-eyed glances. "What?" Pamela asked, raising her voice to be heard over the music.

"You heard me," I yelled back at her. "You want my help? I need to make sure you're legit."

Jonathan Herzberg must have been a pretty desperate man, since, without another word, he peeled off his sports coat. Pamela was slower to untuck her Camp Wawasee oxford T.

"I don't understand," she said as I went around the office, feeling under countertops and lifting up plants and the phone and stuff and looking underneath them. "What's going on?"

Jonathan was a little swifter. He'd completely unbuttoned his shirt, and now he held it open, to show me that nothing was taped to his surprisingly hairless chest.

"She wants to make sure we're not wearing wires," he explained to Pamela.

She continued to look bewildered, but she finally lifted her shirt up enough for me to get a peek underneath. She kept her back to Mr. Herzberg while she did this, and after I'd gotten a look at her bra, I could see why. It was kind of see-through, quite sexy-looking for a camp director and all. I don't know much about bras, not having much of a need for one myself, but couldn't help being impressed by Pamela's.

When they had both proved they weren't wearing transmitters, and I had determined that the place wasn't bugged, I switched the radio off. Then, holding up Keely's photo, I said, "I have to keep this awhile."

"Does this mean you're going to help?" Mr. Herzberg asked eagerly, as he buttoned up again. "Find Keely, I mean?"

"Just give your digits to Pamela," I said, putting Keely's photo in my pocket. "You'll be hearing from me."

Pamela, looking kind of moist-eyed, went, "Oh, Jess. Jess, I'm so glad. Thank you. Thank you so much."

I'm not one for the mushy stuff, and I could feel a big wave of it coming on—mostly from Pamela's direction, but Keely's dad didn't look exactly stone-faced—so I got out of there, and fast.

I would say I'd gotten approximately five or six steps down the hall before I began to have some serious misgivings about what I'd just done. I mean, okay, Pamela had seen some papers giving the guy custody, but that didn't really mean anything. Courts award custody to bad parents all the time. How was I supposed to know whether the story he'd told me about his wife was true?

Simple. I was going to have to check it out.

Great. Not like I didn't have enough to do. Like, for instance, look out for a cabinful of little boys, and, oh yeah, practice for my private lesson with Professor Le Blanc, flutist extraordinaire.

I was wondering how on earth I was going to accomplish all of this—find Keely Herzberg and make sure she really wanted to go back to living with her dad, keep Shane from killing Lionel, and brush up on my fingering for Professor Le Blanc—when I noticed that the secretary whose phone I'd borrowed was in her seat.

And oh, my God, she looked just like John Wayne!

I'm not joking! She looked like a man, and *she* had a boyfriend. Not just any boyfriend, either, but one who raced cars for a living.

I ask you, what is wrong with this picture? Not like unattractive people don't deserve to have boyfriends, but hello, I have been told by several people—and not just by my mother, either—that I am fairly attractive. But do *I* have a boyfriend?

That would be a big N-O.

But Ms. John Wayne over here, she not only has a boyfriend, but a totally hot one, who drives race cars.

Okay. There is so not a God. That's all I have to say about that.

CHAPTER

7

"**H**ey." I put my tray down next to Ruth's. "I need to talk to you."

Ruth was sitting with the girls of Tulip Tree Cottage. They were all eating the same thing for lunch: a large salad, dressing on the side; chicken breasts with the skin removed; cottage cheese; melon slices; and raspberry sherbet for dessert. I am not even joking.

Not that the boys of Birch Tree Cottage were any different. They were following their counselor's example, too. Only their trays were loaded down with pizza, Tater Tots, coleslaw, baked beans, peanut butter bars, macaroni and cheese, ice cream sandwiches, and chocolate chip cookies.

Hey, I'd missed dinner and breakfast. I was hungry, all right?

Ruth looked down at my tray and then glanced quickly away, with a shudder.

"Is it about your saturated fat intake?" she wanted to know. "Because if you keep eating like that, your heart is going to explode."

"You know I have a high metabolism," I said. "Now, listen, this is serious. I might need to borrow your car."

Ruth had been delicately sipping her glass of Diet Coke. When I said the words "your car," she sprayed what was in her mouth all over the little girl sitting opposite her.

"Oh, my God," Ruth said as she leaned across the table to mop up the soda from the little girl's face. "Oh, Shawanda, I am so sorry—"

Shawanda went, "That's okay, Ruth," in this worshipful voice. Like getting sprayed in your face by your counselor was this big honor or something.

"Jeez." Ruth turned to me. "Are you high? You think I'm going to let you borrow my car? You don't even have a license!"

I know it sounds hard to believe, but Ruth was telling the truth. I don't have a driver's license. I am probably the only sixteen-year-old in the state of Indiana without one.

And it's not because I can't drive. I am a good driver, I really am. Better, probably, than Ruth, when it comes down to it.

I just have this one little problem.

Not even a problem, really. More like a need.

A need for speed.

"Absolutely not," Ruth said, spearing a melon wedge and stuffing it into her mouth. Ruth and I have been best friends since kindergarten, so it's not like we ever bother being polite around one another. Ruth spoke around the food in her mouth. "If you think for one minute I would ever let you touch my car, Miss But-I-Was-Only-Going-Eighty-in-a-Thirty-Five-Mile-an-Hour-Zone, you must be on crack."

"I am not," I hissed at her, conscious that the gazes of all the little residents of Tulip Tree Cottage were upon us, "on crack. I just might need a car tomorrow, is all."

"What for?" Ruth demanded.

I didn't want to just come right out and tell her. Not in front of all those inquisitive little faces. So I said, "A situation might arise."

"Jessica," Ruth said. She only calls me by my full name when she is well and truly disgusted with me. "You know we aren't allowed to leave the campgrounds except on Sunday afternoons, which we get off. Tomorrow, I shouldn't need to remind you, is Tuesday. You can't go anywhere. Not without losing your job. Now what's so all-fired important that you are willing to risk losing your job over it?"

I said, "I think I have management's okay on this one. Come on, Ruth, it will only be for a couple of hours."

Ruth's eyes, behind the lenses of her glasses, widened. "Wait a minute. This isn't . . . this isn't about that, you know, *thing*, is it?"

"That, you know, *thing*" is how Ruth often refers

to my newfound talent. The fact that "you know, *thing*" is pretty much all her fault has never seemed to occur to her. I mean, she was, after all, the person who made me walk home the day of the lightning storm. But whatever.

"Yes," I said. "It is about that, you know, *thing*. Now are you going to let me borrow your car, or not?"

Ruth looked thoughtful. "I'll tell you what. If you can promise we won't get into trouble, I'll take you wherever it is you want to go."

Great. Just what I needed.

Don't get me wrong. Ruth's my best friend, and all. But Ruth isn't what you'd ever call good in a crisis. For example, once Ruth's twin brother, Skip, who is allergic to bees, got stung by one, and Ruth responded by clapping her hands over her ears and running out of the room. Seriously. And she'd been fourteen at the time, fully capable of dialing 911 or whatever.

I tell you, it's enough to make you question the judgment of Camp Wawasee's hiring staff, isn't it?

I went, carefully, "Um, you know what? Just forget about it, okay?" Maybe Pamela would let me borrow her car.

But what if Pamela was in on it? I mean, what if, despite the fact she and Jonathan Herzberg hadn't been wearing wires, the two of them were in cahoots with the Feds? What if this whole thing was an elaborately orchestrated sting set up by my good friends with the FBI?

Which was why I needed a car. I needed to check out the situation for myself first.

And not just because there was a chance this might be a setup, but because, well, Keely had rights, too. One thing I had learned last spring—one thing that had been taught to me, and very emphatically, by a boy named Sean who I'd thought was missing, but who, when I found him, turned out to be exactly where he wanted to be—is that when you are in the missing person business, it is a good idea to make sure the person you are looking for actually wants to be found before you go dragging him or her back to where he or she came from. It just makes sense, you know?

Not that I imagined Jonathan Herzberg was lying. If he wasn't in cahoots with the Feds, I mean.

Still, I sort of wanted to hear Keely's mom's side of the story before turning her over to the cops or whatever. And if she really was in Chicago, well, that was only like an hour north of Lake Wawasee. I could make it there and back in the time it took the kids to finish Handel's *Messiah*. Well, almost, anyway.

I wanted to explain all this to Ruth. I wanted to say, "Ruth, look, Pamela isn't going to fire me if I leave the campgrounds because Pamela's the person who is responsible for this in the first place . . . well, sort of."

But another thing I'd learned last spring is that the less people who know about stuff, the better. Really. Even people like your best friend.

"So what I hear you saying"—I tried talking to Ruth the way we'd learned during counselor training to talk to troubled kids—"is that you would feel uncomfortable loaning me your car."

Ruth said, "You hear me correctly. But I'll be glad to go with you, wherever it is. That is, if you can promise we won't get into trouble."

I ate some mac and cheese and pondered how to get out of this without hurting her feelings.

"No guarantees," I finally said, with a shrug.

"Well," Ruth said. "Then you're going to have to find some other boob to loan you their car. What about Dave? I saw him giving you the eye at the pool this morning."

I straightened up. "You did?" I thought he'd been giving *Ruth* the eye.

"I sure did. You should go for it." Ruth nibbled on a piece of chicken. "Hey, maybe we could double. You know, you and Dave, and me and—" I saw her gaze dart over toward Scott's table, then skitter back toward me. She swallowed. "Well, you know," she said, looking embarrassed. "If things work out."

If things worked out between her and Scott, she meant. She took it for granted things would work out between me and Dave. Ruth seemed to forget that I already liked someone, and it wasn't Dave.

Or maybe she wasn't forgetting. Ruth did not exactly approve of my relationship—such as it was—with Rob Wilkins.

Dave Chen, however, was acceptable. In a big

way. I'd overheard him telling someone he'd gotten a near perfect score on his math PSATs.

I was sitting there, wondering why it felt wrong, somehow, to drag a guy like Dave into my problematic existence, when I had never thought twice about dragging Rob, whom I like a whole lot better than I like Dave, into it, when Ruth suddenly went, "Don't you have your first tutorial this afternoon? Shouldn't you be, oh, I don't know, practicing, or something?"

I took a bite of my pizza. Not bad. Not as good as my dad's, of course, but certainly better than that sorry excuse for pizza they serve at the Hut.

"I prefer for Monsieur Le Blanc to hear me at my worst," I explained. "I mean, you can't improve on perfection."

Ruth just waved at me irritably. "Go sit with your little hellions. They're calling you, you know."

My little hellions were, indeed, calling to me. I picked my tray up and joined the rest of the Birch Trees.

"Jess," Tony said. "Get a load of this."

He belched. The rest of the Birch Trees tittered appreciatively.

"That's nothing. Listen to this." Sam took a long swallow of Coke. He then let out a burp of such length and volume, diners at nearby tables glanced over in admiration. Although pleased by this, Sam modestly refused to take total credit for his accomplishment. "Having a deviated septum helps," he informed us.

Seeing that Dr. Alistair, the camp director, had

glanced our way, I quickly steered the conversation in another direction—toward the new Birch Tree Cottage theme song, which I soon had all of them singing heartily:

Oh, they built the ship Titanic
To sail the ocean blue.
They thought it was a ship
No water could get through.
But on its maiden voyage
An iceberg hit that ship.
Oh it was sad when the great ship went down.

Chorus:
Oh it was sad
So sad
It was sad
It was sad when the great ship went down
To the bottom of the—
Husbands and wives, little children lost their lives
It was sad when the great ship went down
Kerplunk
She sunk
Like junk
Cha-cha-cha

Everything was going along swimmingly until I caught Shane, between verses, shoveling down all of Lionel's ice cream—the one food item of which there were no second helpings served at Camp Wawasee, for the obvious reason that, without this restriction, the campers would eat nothing but mint chocolate chip.

"Shane!" I bellowed. He was so surprised, he dropped the spoon.

"Aw, hell," Shane said, looking down at his ice cream–spattered shirt. "Look what the lesbo made me do."

"That's three, Shane," I informed him calmly.

He looked up at me bewilderedly. "Three what? What are you talking about?"

"Three strikes. You're sleeping on the porch tonight, buddy."

Shane sneered. "Big deal."

Arthur said, "Shane, you dink, that means you're going to miss out on the story."

Shane narrowed his eyes at me. "I am not missing out on the story," he said evenly.

I blinked at Arthur. "What story?"

"You're going to tell us another story tonight, aren't you, Jess?"

All the residents of Birch Tree Cottage swiveled their heads around to stare at me. I said, "Sure. Sure, there'll be another story."

Tony poked Shane. "Ha, ha," he teased. "You're gonna miss it."

Shane was furious.

"You can't do that," he sputtered at me. "If you do that, I'll—I'll—"

"You'll do what, Shane?" I asked in a bored voice.

He narrowed his eyes at me. "I'll tell," he said menacingly.

"Tell what?" Arthur, his mouth full of fries, wanted to know.

"Yeah," I said. "Tell what?"

Because of course I'd forgotten. About Shane barging into my room the night before, and catching me with Taylor's photo. I'd forgotten all about it.

But he wasted no time reminding me.

"You know," he said, his eyes slitted with malice. "*Lightning* girl."

I swallowed the mouthful of pizza I'd been chewing. It was like cardboard going down my throat. And not just because it was cafeteria food.

"Hey," I said, attempting to sound as if I didn't care. "Tell whoever you want. Be my guest."

It was a feint, of course, but it worked, taking the wind right out of his sails. His shoulders slumped and he studied his empty plate meditatively, as if hoping an appropriate reply would appear upon it.

I didn't feel the least bit sorry for him. Little bully. But I wasn't just mad at Shane. I was peeved at Lionel, too. How could he just sit there and let people pick on him like that? Granted Shane outweighed him by fifty pounds or so, but I had bested far bigger adversaries when I'd been Lionel's same age and size.

After lunch, as we were walking toward the music building, where the kids would continue their lessons until free play at three, I tried to impress upon Lionel the fact that, if he didn't stand up for himself, Shane was just going to keep on torturing him.

"But, Jess," Lionel said. He pronounced my name as if it were spelled Jace. "He will pound on me."

"Look, Lionel," I said. "He might pound on you. But you just pound him back, only harder. And go for the nose. Big guys are total babies when it comes to their noses."

Lionel looked dubious. "In my country," he said, trilling his *r*'s musically, "violence is looked upon with disfavor."

"Well, you're in America now," I told him. The other Birch Trees had disappeared into their various practice rooms. Only Lionel and I remained in the atrium, along with a few other people.

"Look," I said to him. "Make a fist."

Lionel did so, making the fatal error of folding his thumb inside his fingers.

"No, no, no," I said. "Hold your thumb outside your fingers, or you'll break it, see, when you smash your knuckles into Shane's face."

Lionel moved his thumb, but said, "I do not think I want to smash Shane's face."

"Sure, you do," I said. "And when you do, you don't want to break your thumb. And remember what I said. Go for the nose. Nasal cartilage breaks easily, and you won't hurt your knuckles as much as if you went for, say, the mouth. Never go for the mouth."

"I do not think," Lionel said, "we have to worry about that."

"Good." I patted him on the shoulder. "Now go to class, before you're late."

Lionel took off, clutching his flute case and looking down, a little warily, at his own fist. From the other side of the atrium, I heard applause. Ruth,

Scott, and Dave were standing there with, of all people, Karen Sue Hanky.

"Way to discharge that volatile situation, Jess," Ruth commented sarcastically.

"Yeah," Scott said with a snicker. "By teaching the kid to throw a punch."

Dave was feigning thoughtfulness. "Funny, I don't remember them teaching us that particular method of conflict resolution in counselor training."

They were joking, of course. But Karen Sue, as usual, was deadly serious.

"I think it's disgraceful," she said. "You teaching a little boy to settle his problems with violence. You should be ashamed of yourself."

I stared at her. "You," I said, "have obviously never been the victim of a bully."

Karen Sue stuck out her chin. "No, because I was taught to resolve my differences with others peacefully, without use of force."

"So in other words," I said, "you've never been the victim of a bully."

Ruth laughed outright, but Scott and Dave both put their hands over their mouths, trying to hide their grins. Karen Sue wasn't fooled, though. She said, "Maybe that's because I don't go around *aggravating* people like you do, Jess."

"Oh, that's nice," I said. "Blame the victim, why don't you?"

Now Scott and Dave had to turn toward the wall, they were laughing so hard. Ruth, of course, didn't bother.

The tips of Karen Sue's ears started turning pink. The way I noticed this is that she was wearing this blue headband—which matched her blue shorts, which matched her blue flute case—and the headband pulled her hair back over her ears, so that it fell into these perfect curls just above her shoulders. Oh, and it also showed off her pearl earrings.

Have I mentioned that Karen Sue Hanky is kind of a girlie-girl?

"Well," she said primly. "If you'll excuse me, I'm going back to my cottage now to put my flute away. I hope you enjoy your tutorial with Professor Le Blanc, Jess. He told me that I play exceptionally."

"Yeah," I muttered. "Exceptionally crappy."

Ruth elbowed me.

"Oh, please," I said. "Her flute isn't even open hole. How good can she be?" Besides, Karen Sue had already flounced out. No way she'd overheard me.

Scott, still chuckling, said, "Listen, Jess. Dave and I had an idea. About this ghost story thing of yours. What do you say to teaming up?"

I eyed them. "What are you talking about?"

"Like our cabins could get together after Pit tonight, and you could tell them all another one of those ghost stories. You know, like the one you told last night, that had your little guys so scared, they wouldn't get out of bed afterwards."

"We could bring our guys over," Dave said, "around nine-thirty."

"Yeah," Scott said, glancing shyly in Ruth's direction. "And maybe your girls would want to come, Ruth."

Ruth looked surprised—and pleased—at the suggestion. But reluctance to subject her girls to the likes of Shane overcame her desire to spend quality time with Scott.

"No way," she said. "I'm not letting any of my girls around that little nightmare."

"Maybe Shane'd behave himself," I ventured, "if we threw some estrogen into the mix." It was an experiment they'd tried during detention back at Ernest Pyle High, with somewhat mixed results.

"Nuh-uh," Ruth said. "You know what that kid did during all-camp rehearsal this morning?"

This I hadn't heard. "What?"

"He opened a trumpet's spit valve all over some Frangipanis."

I winced. Not as bad as I'd feared . . . but not exactly good, either.

"And it wasn't," Ruth went on, "even his instrument. He'd *stolen* it. If you think I'm letting my girls near him, you're nuts."

I figured it was just as well. It wasn't like I had a ghost story on hand that I could tell in the presence of a couple of guys like Scott and Dave. They'd know I was plagiarizing Stephen King right away. And how embarrassing, to be sitting there telling some story with my would-be boyfriend Rob as the hero, in front of those guys.

Dave must have noticed my reluctance, since he said, "We'll bring popcorn."

I could see there was no way of getting out of it. And free popcorn is never anything to be sneered at. So I said, "Well, all right. I guess."

"Awesome." Scott and Dave gave each other high fives.

I winced again, but this time it had nothing to do with Shane. Dave had jostled me so that a sharp corner of Keely Herzberg's photo, tucked into the back pocket of my shorts, jabbed me into remembering that I had a little something else to do tonight, too.

CHAPTER

8

"Paul Huck was a guy who lived down the road from me."

I had figured out a way to not embarrass myself in front of Scott and Dave. I'd abandoned the rehashing of an old Stephen King story and opted for a ghost story my dad used to tell, back when my brothers and I had been little and he'd taken us on camping trips to the Indiana backwoods—trips my mother never went on, since she claimed to be allergic to nature, and most particularly to backwoods.

"He wasn't a very bright guy," I explained to the dozens of rapt little faces in front of me. "In fact, he was kind of dim. He only made it to about the fourth grade before school got too hard for him, so his parents let him stay home after that, since they didn't put much stock in education anyway, on account of none of the Hucks ever amounting to anything with or without having gone to school—"

"Hey." A small, high-pitched voice sounded from behind the closed porch door. "Can I come in now?"

"No," I shouted back. "Now, where was I?"

I went on to relate how Paul Huck had grown into a massive individual, stupid as a corncob, but good at heart.

But really, I wasn't thinking about Paul Huck. I wasn't thinking about Paul Huck at all. I was thinking about what had happened right after I'd agreed to allow Scott and Dave have their cabins stage a mini-invasion on mine. What had happened was, I had gone for my tutorial with Professor Le Blanc.

And I had ended up nearly getting fired.

Again.

And this time, it hadn't been because I'd been making personal use of camp property, or teaching the kids risqué songs.

Then why, you ask? Why would the famous classical flutist Jean-Paul Le Blanc attempt to fire a totally hip—not to mention talented—individual like myself?

Because he had discovered my deepest secret, the one I hold closest to my heart. . . .

No, not that one. Not the fact that I am still very much in possession of my psychic gift. My *other* secret.

What happened was this.

Right after Scott and Dave and Ruth took off, I sauntered over to the practice room where I was supposed to have my lesson with Professor Le Blanc. He was in there, all right. I could tell by the pure, sweet tones emanating from the tiny room. The practice rooms are supposed to be soundproof, and they are . . . but only if you're in one of the rooms. From the hallway, you can hear what's going on behind the door.

And let me tell you, what was going on behind that door was some fine, fine Bach. We're talking flute-playing so elegant, so assured, so . . . well, passionate, it almost brought tears to my eyes. You don't hear that kind of playing in the Ernest Pyle High School Symphonic Orchestra, you get what I'm saying? I was so entranced, I didn't even think to knock on the door to let the professor know I'd arrived. I never wanted that sweet music to end.

But it did end. And then the next thing I knew, the door to the practice room was opening, and Professor Le Blanc emerged. He was saying, "You have a gift. An extraordinary gift. Not to use it would be a crime."

"Yes, Professor," replied a bored voice that, oddly, I recognized.

I looked down, shocked that such lovely music had been coming from the flute of a student, and not the master.

And my jaw sagged.

"Hey, lesbo," Shane said. "Shut the barn door, you're lettin' the flies in."

"Ah," Professor Le Blanc said, spying me. "You two know one another? Oh, yes, of course, Jessica, you are his counselor, I'd forgotten. Then you can do me a very great favor."

I was still staring at Shane. I couldn't help it. That music? That beautiful music? That had been coming from *Shane?*

"Make certain," Professor Le Blanc said, resting his hands on Shane's pudgy shoulders, "that this young man understands how rare a talent like his is. He insists that his mother made him come to Wawasee this summer. That in fact he'd have much preferred to attend baseball camp instead."

"*Football* camp," Shane burst out bitterly. "I don't *want* to play the flute. *Girls* play the flute." He glared at me very fiercely as he said this, as if daring me to contradict him.

I did not. I could not. I was still transfixed. All I could think was *Shane? Shane* played the *flute?* I mean, he'd said he played the *skin* flute. I didn't know he'd been telling the truth . . . well, partially, anyway.

But an actual *flute? Shane* had been the one making that gorgeous—no, not just gorgeous—*magnificent* music on *my* instrument of choice? Shane? *My* Shane?

Professor Le Blanc was shaking his head. "Don't be ridiculous," he said to Shane. "Most of the greatest flutists in the world have been men. And with talent like yours, young man, you might one day be amongst them—"

"Not if I get recruited by the Bears," Shane pointed out.

"Well," Professor Le Blanc said, looking a little taken aback. "Er, maybe not then . . ."

"Is my lesson over?" Shane demanded, craning his neck to get a look at the professor's face.

"Er," Professor Le Blanc said. "Yes, actually, it is."

"Good," Shane said, tucking his flute case beneath his arm. "Then I'm outta here."

And with that, he stalked away.

Professor Le Blanc and I stared after him for a minute or two. Then the instructor seemed to shake himself, and, holding open the door to the practice room for me, said with forced jocularity, "Well, now, let's see what you can do, then, Jessica. Why don't you play something for me?" Professor Le Blanc went to the piano that stood in one corner of the walk-in-closet-sized room, sat down on the bench, and picked up a Palm Pilot. "Anything you like," he said, punching the buttons of the Palm Pilot. "I like to assess my pupil's skill level before I begin teaching."

I opened my flute case and began assembling my instrument, but my mind wasn't on what I was doing. I just couldn't get what I'd heard out of my head. It didn't make sense. It didn't make sense that Shane could play like that. It just didn't seem possible. The kid had played beautifully, movingly, as if he'd been swept away by the notes, each one of which had rung out with angelic—almost aching—purity. The same Shane who had stuck an entire hamburger in his mouth at lunch—I'd sat there and watched him do it—bun and all, then swallowed it, practically whole, just because Arthur had dared him to. That same Shane. That Shane could play like *that*.

And he didn't even care. He'd wanted to go to football camp.

He'd been lying. He cared. No one could play like that and not care. No one.

I put my own flute to my lips, and began to play. Nothing special. Green Day. "Time of Our Lives." I jazzed it up a little, since it's a relatively simple little song. But all I could think about was Shane. There had to be depths, *wells* of untapped emotion in that boy, to make him capable of producing such music.

And all he wanted to do was play football.

Professor Le Blanc looked up from his Palm Pilot at some point during my recital. When I was through, he said, "Play something else, please."

I launched into an old standby. "Fascinating Rhythm." Always a crowd-pleaser. At least it pleased my dad, when I was practicing at home. I usually played it at double time, to get it over with. I did so now.

The question was, how could a kid who could play like that be such a total and complete pain in the butt? I mean, how was it possible that the person who'd played such hauntingly beautiful music, and the person who this morning had told Lionel he'd dipped his toothbrush in the toilet—after, of course, Lionel had started using it—be one and the same individual?

Professor Le Blanc was rooting through his briefcase, which he'd left on top of the piano.

"Here," he said. "Now this." He dropped a book of sheet music onto the stand in front of my chair.

Brahms. Symphony Number 1. What was he trying to do, put me to sleep? It was an insult. We'd played that my freshman year, for God's sake. My fingers flew over the key holes. Open, of course. My instrument was practically an antique, handed down from some obscure member of the Mastriani clan who'd gotten it under questionable circumstances. Yeah, okay, so my flute was probably hot.

The thing I couldn't figure out was what was God—and I'm not saying I'm so all-fired sure there is one, but for argument's sake, let's say there is—thinking, giving a kid like Shane talent like that? Seriously. Why had he been given this incredible gift of music, when clearly, he'd have been happier tearing down a field with a ball in his arms?

I tell you, if that's not proof there is a God, and that he or she has one heck of a wacked-out sense of humor, I don't know what is.

"Stop." Professor Le Blanc took the Brahms away and put another music book in front of me.

Beethoven. Symphony Number 3.

I don't know how long I sat there looking at it. Maybe a full minute before I was able to rouse myself from my Shane-induced stupor and go, "Um, Professor? Yeah, look, I don't know this piece."

Professor Le Blanc was still sitting on the piano bench, his arms folded across his chest. He had put away the Palm Pilot, and was now watching me intently. The fact that he was, in fact, a bit of a hottie, did not make this any pleasanter than it sounds. He looked a little like a hawk, one of those hawks you

see all the time, wheeling in tighter and tighter cir-
cles above something in a cornfield, making you
wonder what the stupid bird is looking at down
there. Is it a field mouse, or the decomposing body of
a coed?

Professor Le Blanc said, enunciating carefully, "I
know you don't know this piece, Jess. I want to see if
you can play it."

I just stared at it.

"Well," I said after a while. "I probably could. If
you would maybe just hum my part first?"

He didn't look surprised by my request. He shook
his head so that his kind of longish, curly brown
hair—definitely longer than mine, anyway—swung
around.

"No," he said. "I do not hum. Begin, please."

I squirmed uncomfortably in my seat. "It's just," I
explained, "usually, back home, my orchestra teacher,
he kind of hums the whole thing out for us first, and I
really—"

"Aha!"

Professor Le Blanc yelled so loud, I almost dropped
my flute. He pointed a long, accusing finger at me.

"*You*," he said, in tones of mingled triumph and
horror, "*cannot read music*."

I felt my own ears turning as pink as Karen Sue's
had out in the atrium. Only not just pink. Red. My
ears were burning. My face was burning. It was air-
conditioned enough in that practice room that you
practically needed a winter parka, but me, I was on
fire.

"That isn't true," I said, trying to appear casual. Yeah, real easy to do with a face that was turning fire-engine red. "That note right there, for instance." I pointed at the music. "That's an eighth note. And over here, that's a whole note."

"But what note," Professor Le Blanc demanded, "is it?"

My shoulders slumped. I was so busted.

"Look," I said. "I don't *need* to read music. I just have to hear the piece once, and I—"

"—and you know how to play it. Yes, yes, I know. I know all about you people. You I-hear-it-once-and-I-know-it people." He shook his head disgustedly at me. "Does Dr. Alistair know about this?"

I felt my feet beginning to sweat inside my Pumas, that's how freaked out he had me.

"No," I said. "You aren't going to tell him, are you?"

"Not going to tell him?" Professor Le Blanc leaped up from the piano bench. "Not going to tell Dr. Alistair that one of his counselors is musically *illiterate?*"

He bellowed the last word. Anyone passing outside the door could have heard. I went, in a small voice, "Please, Professor Le Blanc. Don't turn me in. I'll learn to read this piece. I promise."

"I do not want you to learn to read this piece." Professor Le Blanc was on his feet now, and pacing the length of the practice room. Which, only being about six feet by six feet, wasn't very far. "You should be able to read *all* pieces. How can you be so lazy? Simply because you can hear a piece once and then play it, you use this as an excuse never to learn to read music? You ought to be ashamed. You ought to be sent back to where you came from and made to work there at the IG of A as a sack girl."

I licked my lips. I couldn't help it. My mouth had gone completely dry.

"Um, Professor?" I said.

He was still pacing and breathing kind of hard. In school, they made us read this book about this guy named Heathcliff who liked this loser chick named Cathy, who didn't like him back, and I swear to God, Professor Le Blanc kind of reminded me of old Heathcliff, the way he was huffing and puffing about something that really boiled down to nothing.

"*What?*" he yelled at me.

I swallowed. "It's bag girl." When he only gazed at me uncomprehendingly, I said, "You said I'd have to work as a sack girl. But it's called a bag girl."

Professor Le Blanc pointed toward the door. "*Out,*" he roared.

I was shocked. The whole thing was totally unfair. In the movies, when somebody finds out the other person can't read, they're always filled with all this compassion and try to help the poor guy. Like Jane Fonda helped Robert De Niro when she found out he couldn't read in this really boring movie my mom made me watch with her once. I couldn't believe Professor Le Blanc was being so unfeeling. My case, if you thought about it, was really quite tragic.

I figured I'd make a play for his heartstrings . . . if he had any, which I doubted.

"Professor," I said. "Look. I know I deserve to get thrown out of here and all, but really, that's partly why I took this gig. I mean, I completely realize my inability to read music is hampering my growth as an artist, and I was really hoping this was my big chance to, you know, rectify that."

I totally did not believe he would go for this crap, but to my never-ending relief, he did. I don't know why. Maybe it was because I was trembling. Not because I was nervous or anything. I was, but not that much. I mean, it wasn't like the steam table held that much horror for me. It was just because it was about thirty degrees in there.

But I guess Professor Le Blanc thought I was suitably cowed or whatever, since he finally said he wouldn't turn me in to Dr. Alistair. Although he wasn't very gracious about it, I must say. He told me that, since his class schedule was completely filled, he didn't have the time to teach me to read music *and* prepare my piece for the concert at the end of the summer. I was like, fine, I don't want to be in the stupid concert anyway, but he got all offended, because the concert's supposed to be, you know, what all of us are working toward for the six weeks we're here.

Finally, we agreed I'd meet him three times a week at seven A.M.—yes, that would be seven in the morning—so he could teach me what I needed to know. I tried to point out that seven A.M. was the

Polar Bear swim, which also happened to be the only time I could realistically bathe, but he so didn't care.

God. Musicians. So temperamental.

While I was sitting there back in Birch Tree Cottage, thinking about how close I'd been to getting fired, and talking about Paul Huck, I looked out at all the kids in front of me and wondered how many of them were going to grow up to be Professor Le Blancs. Probably all of them. And that saddened me. Because it seemed like they were never even going to get the chance to be anything else, if they only got two hours of free time a day to play.

Except Shane, of course. Shane, the only one of the kids at Camp Wawasee for Gifted Child Musicians who probably could make a living as a musician one day if he wanted to, clearly didn't. Want to, I mean. He wanted to be a football player.

And you know, I could sort of relate to that. I knew what a pain it was to have a gift you'd never, ever asked for.

"—so Paul Huck got jobs around the neighborhood," I went on, "mowing lawns and doing people's yardwork in the summer, and chopping firewood in the winter. And pretty much nobody noticed him, but when they did, they thought he was, you know, a pretty nice guy. Not a whole lot upstairs, though."

I glanced at Scott and Dave. They were sitting on the windowsill. In a few minutes, I would give the signal, and one of them would sneak into the kitchen to say his line.

"But there was actually a lot going on upstairs in Paul Huck's head," I said. "Because Paul Huck, while he was in people's yards, digging up their tree stumps or whatever, he was watching them. And the person he liked to watch most of all was a girl named Claire Lippman, who, every day during the summer, liked to climb out onto her porch roof and sunbathe in this little bitty bikini."

It was kind of disturbing the way real people crept into my made-up stories. In my dad's version, the girl was named Debbie. But Claire, who'd be a senior at Ernie Pyle this year, just seemed to fit somehow.

"Paul fell for Claire," I went on. "And Paul fell hard. He thought about Claire while he ate breakfast every morning. He thought about Claire while he was riding his tractor mower every afternoon. He thought about Claire when he was eating his dinner at night. He thought about Claire while he was lying in bed after a long day's work. Paul Huck thought about Claire Lippman *all* the time.

"But." I looked out at all the little faces turned toward me. "Claire Lippman didn't think about Paul Huck at breakfast. She didn't think about him while she was sunning herself on her porch roof every afternoon. She didn't think about him while she ate her dinner, and she certainly never thought about him before she fell asleep at night. Claire Lippman never thought about Paul Huck at all, because she barely even knew Paul Huck existed. To Claire, Paul was just the handyman who knocked squirrels' nests out of her chimney every spring, and who scooped the dead opossums out of this decorative little well she had in her backyard. And that was it."

I could feel the crowd getting restless. It was time to start getting to the gore.

Eventually, I told them, Paul got desperate. He knew if he was ever going to win Claire's heart, he had to act. So one spring day when he was cleaning out Claire's gutters, he got an idea. He decided he was going to tell Claire how he felt.

"Just as this occurred to Paul, Claire appeared in the window right where he was cleaning out the gutter. This seemed to Paul like the perfect time to say what he was going to say. But just as he was about to tap on the window, Claire started taking her clothes off." This caused some tittering that I ignored. "See, the room she was in was the bathroom, and she was getting ready to take a shower. She didn't notice Paul there in the window . . . at first. And Paul, well, he didn't know what to do. He had never seen a naked woman before, let alone the love of his life, Claire. So he just froze there on the ladder, totally incapable of moving.

"So when Claire happened to glance at the window, just as she was about to get in the shower, and saw Paul there, she was so startled, she let out a scream so loud, it almost made Paul fall off the ladder he was on.

"But Claire didn't stop with one scream. She was so startled, she kept right on screaming. People outside heard the screaming, and they looked up, and they saw Paul Huck looking through Claire Lippman's bathroom window, and, well, they didn't know he was there to clean the gutters. He had always been a weird guy, who lived at home with his parents even though he was in his twenties, and who talked like a nine-year-old. Maybe he'd flipped out or something. So they started yelling, too, and Paul was so scared, with all the yelling and everything going on, he jumped down from the ladder and ran for all he was worth.

"Paul didn't know what he'd done, but he figured it had to be pretty bad, if it had made so many people mad at him. All he knew was that, whatever it was he'd done, it was probably bad enough that someone had called the police, and if the police came, they'd put him in jail. So Paul didn't go home, because he figured that'd be the first place people would look for him. Instead, he ran to the outskirts of town, where there was this cave. Everyone was scared to go into this cave, because bats and stuff lived in there. But Paul was more afraid of the police than he was of bats, so he ducked into that cave, and he stayed there, all the way until it got dark.

"Now, once Claire got over being startled, she realized what had happened, and she felt pretty bad about it. But she didn't want to admit to anyone that it had been her mistake—that she'd asked Paul to clean her gutters, and that's what he'd been doing on that ladder. Because then she'd look like a big idiot. So she kept that information to herself, and let everyone think Paul was a Peeping Tom."

I went on to describe how Paul, scared for his life,

stayed in that cave. He stayed there all night, and all the next day, and the next night, too. I explained how by then, Paul's parents were really worried. They had called the police to help them look, but that just made things worse, because one time Paul came out of the cave, to see if people were still looking for him, and he saw a sheriff's cruiser go by. That just drove him deeper back into the cave, where when he was thirsty, he drank cave water.

"But there was no food in the cave," I said. "And Paul couldn't come out to buy any, because he might get caught. Eventually, he got so hungry, well, he just lost his mind. He saw a bat, and he grabbed it, ripped its head off, and ate it raw."

This elicited some groans of disgust.

And that, I told the boys, was the beginning of Paul's descent into madness. Very soon, he was living on nothing but cave water and bat meat. He lost all this weight, and started growing this long, matted beard. He couldn't wash his hair because he didn't have any shampoo, so it started getting all filled with twigs and dirt. His clothes became tattered and hung off him like rags. But still, he wouldn't come out of the cave, because he couldn't face the shame of whatever it was he'd done to Claire.

Time went by. Winter came. Soon Paul ran out of bats to eat. He had no choice but to leave the cave at night, and root through people's garbage for old chicken bones and rotten milk, so he wouldn't starve. Sometimes, little children would wake up in the night and see him, and they'd tell their parents the next morning about the strange, long-haired man they'd seen in the backyard, and their parents would say, "Stop telling lies."

But the children knew what they'd seen.

More time went by. One night, Paul Huck was going through someone's garbage when he came across a newspaper. Newspapers didn't interest Paul much, on account of his not being able to read. But this one had a picture on it. He squinted at the picture in the moonlight and realized it was a picture of his old love, Claire Lippman. He didn't need to know how to read in order to figure out why Claire's picture was in the paper. In the photo, she was dressed in a wedding gown and veil. Claire Lippman had gotten married.

Paul, crazy as he was now, couldn't think like a normal person—not that he'd ever been able to before. But after a steady diet of bats and garbage, which was all he'd had to eat for the past few years, he'd gotten much worse. So what seemed to Paul like a really good idea—he ought to give Claire a wedding present, to show there were no hard feelings—well, that just wouldn't have occurred to a normal person.

"What was worse," I said, "Paul's idea of a wedding present was to go through all the yards in the town and pick every rose he could find. He did this, of course, in the middle of the night, and all over town children woke up and looked out the window and said, 'There's Paul Huck again,' and they wondered what he was going to do with all the roses.

"What Paul did with all the roses was, he piled

them up on Claire Lippman's front porch, so she'd see them first thing when she came out of her house to go to work."

And there, I told the kids, for the first time ever, an adult woke up and heard Paul Huck. It was Claire's new husband, Simon, who was a stranger to the town. He didn't know who Paul Huck was. All Simon knew was, when he came downstairs into the kitchen to get a glass of milk before going back to sleep, he saw this gigantic, shaggy-haired man, covered in dirt and blood—because the roses' thorns had cut Paul everywhere he touched them—standing on his front porch. Simon didn't even think about what he was doing. Since he was in the kitchen, he grabbed the first thing he saw that he could use as a weapon—a carving knife—and went to the front door, threw it open, and said, "Who the hell are you?"

"Paul was so surprised that someone was speaking to him—no one had said a word to him, not in five long years—that he spun around, just as he'd been about to leave the porch. Simon didn't understand that Paul was just startled. He thought this giant, hairy, bloody guy was coming after him. So Simon swung the carving knife, and it caught Paul just beneath the chin, and *whoosh* . . . it cut off his head. Paul Huck," I said, "was dead."

Silence followed this.

I went on to describe how Claire's husband, in a panic after seeing what he had done, ran inside the house to call the police. Hearing all the commotion,

Claire woke up and came downstairs. She went out onto the porch. The first thing she saw was all the roses. The second thing she saw was this great big bloody body laying on top of them. The last thing she saw was a head, almost buried in the roses.

And even though the head had this long beard, and the eyes were all rolled back, Claire recognized Paul Huck. And she put together the roses and the fact that it was Paul and she knew that her husband had just killed the man that, because of her, had been living like an animal for five long years.

Claire wouldn't let Simon call the police. He had killed, she insisted, an innocent man. Paul had never meant to hurt either of them. If word got out about this, Claire and her new husband—who was this very important surgeon—were going to be socially ruined in town, and she knew it. She explained all this to Simon. They had, she said, to hide the body, and pretend like nothing had happened.

Simon was disgusted, but like Claire, he enjoyed his status high at the top of the town's social ladder. So he made a deal with her: he'd get rid of Paul's body, if Claire got rid of the head.

Claire agreed. So while Simon wrapped Paul's body in sheets—so he wouldn't bleed all over the back of his new car while Simon drove over to the lake, where he intended to dump the body—Claire lifted up the head and threw it in the first place she thought of: down the well in her backyard.

When Simon got back from the lake, the two of them

cleaned up all the blood and roses. Then, exhausted, they went back to bed.

Everything seemed to go okay at first. Nobody except the children of the town had ever believed Paul Huck was still alive anyway, so nobody noticed that he was gone. Little by little, Claire and Simon were able to put from their minds what they had done. Their lives went back to normal.

Until the first full moon after Paul's murder. That night, Claire and Simon were awakened from their sleep by a moaning they heard coming from the backyard. At first they thought it was the wind. But it seemed to be moaning words. And those words were, "Where's . . . my . . . head?"

They thought they must have been hearing things. But then, sounding even closer than the first moan, they heard the words, "Down . . . in . . . the . . . well."

Claire and Simon put on their bathrobes and hurried downstairs. Looking out into their backyard, they got the shock of their lives. For there, in the moonlight, they saw a horrifying sight: Paul Huck's headless body, all covered with lake weeds and dripping wet, moaning, "Where's . . . my . . . head?"

And, from deep inside the well, the echoing reply: "Down . . . in . . . the . . . well!"

Claire and her husband both went instantly insane. They ran from the house that night, and they never went back, not even to move out their stuff. They hired a moving company to do it for them. They put the house up for sale.

"But you know what?" I looked at all the faces

gazing at me in the soft glow of my single flashlight. "No one ever bought the house. It was like everyone could sense that there was something wrong with it. No one ever bought it, and little by little, it began to fall apart. Vandals threw rocks through its windows, and rats moved in, and bats, just like the ones Paul used to eat, lived in the attic. It is still empty, to this day. And on nights when the moon is full, if you go into the backyard, you can still hear the wind moaning, just like Paul Huck: 'Where's . . . my . . . head?' "

From the dark kitchen came a deep, ghostly wail: "Down . . . in . . . the . . . well!"

Several things happened at once. The boys all screamed. Scott, grinning, emerged from the kitchen. And the front door burst open, and Shane, panting and white-faced, cried, "Did you hear that? Did you hear that? It's him, it's Paul Huck! He's coming to get us! Please don't make me sleep outside, I promise I'll be good from now on, I promise!"

And with that, I began to see a little—just a little—more clearly how it might be possible for a kid like Shane to make that beautiful music.

CHAPTER

9

When I woke up the next morning, I knew where Keely Herzberg was.

Not that there was much I could do with the information. I mean, it wasn't like I was going to run over to Pamela's office and tell her what I knew. Not yet, anyway. I needed to check the situation out, make sure Keely wanted to be found.

And, thanks to Paul Huck, I knew exactly how I was going to do it.

Well, not thanks to Paul Huck, exactly. But thanks to the fact that I'd had Scott and Dave and their kids over the night before, I was a lot more savvy to the whole phone situation than I'd been before. It turns out all the counselors have cell phones. Seriously. Everyone except Ruth and me . . . and Karen Sue Hanky, I suppose, since she'd never do anything that might be construed as breaking the rules.

I don't know why Ruth and I are so out of it. We're like the only two sixteen-year-old girls in Indiana without cell phones. What is wrong with our parents? You would think they would want us to have cell phones, so that we could call them when we're going to be out late, or whatever.

But then, we're never out late, because we never really get invited anywhere. That would be on account of our being orchestra nerds. Oh, and on account of my *issues*, too, I guess.

But everybody else on the camp counseling staff had cell phones. They'd been making and receiving calls all week, just keeping them on vibrate and picking up out of Pamela's and Dr. Alistair's sight.

So now, thanks to my scaring their charges so thoroughly the night before that they apparently did everything their counselors asked them to afterward—like go to sleep—both Scott and Dave were eager, when I asked them at breakfast, to lend me their phones.

I took Dave's, since it had less buttons and looked less intimidating. Then I ducked out of the dining hall and went to the Pit, which was empty this time of day. I figured reception there was bound to be good. . . .

And it didn't seem likely that if the Feds were still monitoring my activities they'd be able to sneak up on me without me noticing.

Rob's phone rang about five times before he picked up.

"Hey, it's me," I said. And then since, for all I

knew, there might be dozens of girls calling him before nine in the morning, I added, "Jess."

"I know it's you," Rob said. He didn't sound sleepy or anything. He usually opened the garage for his uncle, so he gets up pretty early. "What's up? How are things up there at band camp?"

"It's orchestra camp."

"Whatever. How's it going?"

What is it about Rob's voice that makes me feel all shivery, the way I'd felt in the super air-conditioned practice room the day before . . . only inside, not outside? I don't know. But I strongly suspect it had something to do with the *L* word.

Though it was just plain wrong, my having fallen so hard for a guy who so clearly wanted to have nothing to do with me. Why couldn't he see we were made for each other? I mean, we'd met in detention, for God's sake. Need I say more?

"Things are okay," I said. "Except I sort of have this problem."

"Oh, yeah? What's that?"

I tried to picture what Rob looked like, sitting there in his kitchen—he and his mom only have one phone, and it's in the kitchen. I figured he was probably wearing jeans. I'd never seen him in anything but jeans. Which was just as well, because he looks extraordinarily fine in them. It was like his butt had been designed to be molded by a pair of Levi's, his broad shoulders contoured specifically to fill out that leather jacket he always wore when he rode his motorcycle.

And the rest of him wasn't that bad, either.

"Well," I said, trying not to think about the way his curly dark hair, which was usually in need of a trim, had felt against my cheek the last time he'd let me kiss him. It had been a long time ago. Too long. Oh, God, why couldn't I be just a couple years older?

"Look," I said. "Here's the thing." And I told him, briefly, about Jonathan Herzberg.

"So," I concluded, "I just need a ride into Chicago to sort of check out the situation, and I know you have work and all, but I was kind of wondering if, when you get a day off, or whatever, you wouldn't mind—"

"Mastriani," he said. He didn't sound mad or anything, even though I was trying to use him . . . and pretty blatantly, too. "You're *four hours* away."

I winced. I'd been hoping he wouldn't remember that until after he'd said yes. See, in my imagination, when I'd rehearsed this call, Rob had been so excited to hear from me, he'd hopped right onto his bike and come over, no questions asked.

In real life, however, guys ask questions.

"I know it's far," I said. You dope. What did you expect? He said he doesn't want to go out with you. When are you going to get that through your thick skull?

"You know what?" I said. "Never mind. I can just get somebody else—"

"I don't like it," Rob said. I thought he meant he didn't like my asking somebody else to drive me, and I got kind of excited for a minute, but then he went, "Why the hell did your brother tell this guy where you were in the first place?"

I sighed. Rob had never met Douglas. Or anybody in my family, for that matter, except my dad, and that was just for a minute once. I don't think any of them would be that thrilled by the fact that I was in love with a guy I'd met in detention.

Or that the reason—at least the one that he gives me—that we aren't going out is that he's on probation, and doesn't want to screw it up by dating a minor.

My life has gotten seriously complicated, I swear.

"How do you know," Rob demanded, "that this isn't a setup by those agents who were after you last spring? I mean, it very well could be a trap, Mastriani. They might have arranged this whole thing as a way to prove you lied when you said you didn't have your powers anymore."

"I know," I said. "That's why I want to check it out first. But I'll just get someone else to take me. It's no big deal."

"What about Ruth?" Rob had only met Ruth once or twice. He had called her the fat chick the first time he'd ever referred to her, but he'd quickly learned I don't let people dis my best friend that way. Nor do I let Ruth call Rob what she calls everybody in our town who lives outside the city limits: a Grit. If Rob and I ever did start going out, there'd definitely be a little friction between the two of them. So much for me being able to tell he secretly loves me by the way he treats my friends. "Can't Ruth take you?"

"No," I said. I didn't want to get into the whole Ruth-being-no-good-in-a-crisis thing. "Look, don't worry about it. I'll find someone. It's no big deal."

"What do you mean, you'll find someone?" Rob sounded exasperated with me, which he didn't have any right to be. It's not like he's my boyfriend, or anything. "Who are you going to find?"

"There are a couple people," I said, "with cars. I'll just have to see if I can get any of them to take me, that's all."

Dave appeared suddenly at the top of the stairs down into the Pit. He called, "Hey, Jess, you almost through? I gotta take my crew on over to the music building now."

"Oh," I said. "Yeah, just a minute." Into the phone, I said, "Look, I gotta go. This guy loaned me his phone, and I have to give it back now, because he's leaving."

"What guy?" Rob demanded. "There's guys there? I thought it was a camp for kids."

"Well, it is," I said. Was it my imagination, or did he sound . . . well, unsettled? "But there's guy counselors and all."

"What's a *guy* doing," Rob wanted to know, "working at a band camp for little kids? They let *guys* do that?"

"Well, sure," I said. "Why not? Hey, wait a minute." I squinted up at Dave. Even though it wasn't quite nine yet, you could tell from the way the sun was beating down that it was going to be a scorcher. "Hey, Dave," I called. "You got a car, right?"

"Yeah," Dave said. "Why? You planning on staging a breakout?"

Into the phone, I said, "You know what, Rob? I think I—"

But Rob was already talking. And what he was saying, I was surprised to hear, was, "I'll pick you up at one."

I went, totally confused, "You'll what? What are you talking about?"

"I'll be there at one," Rob said again. "Where will you be? Give me directions."

Bemused, I gave Rob directions, and agreed to meet him at a bend in the road just past the main gates into the camp. Then I hung up, still wondering what had made him change his mind.

I trudged up the steps to where Dave stood, and handed him back his phone.

"Thanks," I said. "You're a lifesaver."

Dave shrugged. "You really need a ride somewhere?"

"Not anymore," I said. "I—"

And that's when it hit me. Why Rob had been so blasé about my going away for seven weeks, and why, just now on the phone, he'd changed his mind about coming up:

He hadn't thought there'd be guys here.

Seriously. He'd thought it was just going to be me and Ruth and about two hundred little kids, and that was it. It had never occurred to him there might be guys my own age hanging around.

That was the only explanation I could think of, anyway, for his peculiar behavior.

Except, of course, that explanation made no sense whatsoever. Because for it to be true, it would mean Rob would have to like me, you know, *that way*, and I was pretty sure he didn't. Otherwise, he wouldn't care so much about his stupid probation officer, and what he has to say on the matter.

Then again, the prospect of jail *is* a pretty daunting one. . . .

"Jess? Are you all right?"

I shook myself. Dave was staring at me. I had drifted off into Rob Wilkins dreamland right in front of him.

"Oh," I said. "Yeah. Fine. Thanks. No, I don't need a ride anymore. I'm good."

He slipped his cell phone back into his pocket. "Oh. Okay."

"You know what I do need, though, Dave?" I asked.

Dave shook his head. "No. What?"

I took a deep breath. "I need someone to keep an eye on my kids this afternoon," I said, in a rush. "Just for a little while. I, um, might be tied up with something."

Dave, unlike Ruth, didn't give me a hard time. He just shrugged and went, "Sure."

My jaw sagged. "Really? You don't mind?"

He shrugged again. "No. Why should I mind?"

We started back toward the dining hall. As we approached it, I noticed most of the residents of Birch

Tree Cottage had finished breakfast and were outside, gathered around one of the campground dogs.

"It's a grape," Shane was saying, conversationally, to Lionel. "Go ahead and eat it."

"I do not believe it is a grape," Lionel replied. "So I do not think I will, thank you."

"No, really." Shane pointed at something just beneath the dog's ear. "In America, that's where grapes grow."

When I got close enough, of course, I saw what it was they were talking about. Hanging off one of the dog's ears was a huge, blood-engorged tick. It did look a bit like a grape, but not enough, I thought, to fool even the most gullible foreigner.

"Shane," I said, loudly enough to make him jump.

"What?" Shane widened his baby blues at me innocently. "I wasn't doing anything, Jess. Honest."

Even I was shocked at this bold-faced lie. "You were so," I said. "You were trying to make Lionel eat a tick."

The other boys giggled. In spite of the fright Shane had gotten the night before—and I had ended up letting him sleep inside; even I wasn't mean enough to make him sleep on the porch after the whole Paul Huck thing—he was back to his old tricks.

Next time, I was going to make him spend the night on a raft in the middle of the lake, I swear to God.

"Apologize," I commanded him.

Shane said, "I don't see why I should have to apologize for something I didn't do."

"Apologize," I said, again. "And then get that tick off that poor dog."

This was my first mistake. I should have removed the tick myself.

My second mistake was in turning my back on the boys to roll my eyes at Dave, who'd been watching the entire interaction with this great big grin on his face. Last night, he and Scott had confided to me that all the other counselors had placed bets on who was going to win in the battle of wills between Shane and me. The odds were running two to one in Shane's favor.

"Sorry, Lie-oh-nell," I heard Shane say.

"Make sure you mention this," I said, to Dave, "to your—"

The morning air was pierced by a scream.

I spun around just in time to see Lionel, his white shirt now splattered with blood, haul back his fist and plunge it, with all the force of his sixty-five pounds or so, into Shane's eye. He'd been aiming, I guess, for the nose, but missed.

Shane staggered back, clearly more startled by the blow than actually hurt by it. Nevertheless, he immediately burst into loud, babyish sobs, and, both hands pressed to the injured side of his face, wailed in a voice filled with shock and outrage, "He *hit* me! Jess, he *hit* me!"

"Because he make the tick explode on me!" Lionel declared, holding out his shirt for me to see.

"All right," I said, trying to keep my breakfast down. "That's enough. Get to class, both of you."

Lionel, horrified, said, "I cannot go to class like this!"

"I'll bring you a new shirt," I said. "I'll go back to the cabin and get one and bring it to you while you're in music theory."

Mollified, the boy picked up his flute case and, with a final glare in Shane's direction, stomped off to class.

Shane, however, was not so easily calmed.

"He should get a strike!" he shouted. "He should get a strike, Jess, for hitting me!"

I looked at Shane like he was crazy. I actually think that at that moment, he *was* crazy.

"Shane," I said. "You sprayed him with tick blood. He had every right to hit you."

"That's not fair," Shane shouted, his voice catching on a sob. "That's not *fair!*"

"For God's sake, Shane," I said, with some amusement. "It's a good thing you went to orchestra camp instead of football camp this summer, if you're gonna cry every time someone pokes you in the eye."

This had not, perhaps, been the wisest thing to say, under the circumstances. Shane's face twisted with emotion, but I couldn't tell if it was embarrassment or pain. I was a little shocked that I'd managed to hurt his feelings. It was actually kind of hard to believe a kid like Shane *had* feelings.

"I didn't *choose* to come to this stupid camp," Shane roared at me. "My mother *made* me! She wouldn't *let* me go to football camp. She was afraid I'd hurt my stupid hands and not be able to play the stupid flute anymore."

I dried up, hearing this. Because suddenly, I could see Shane's mother's point of view. I mean, the kid could play.

"Shane," I said gently. "Your mom's right. Professor Le Blanc, too. You have an incredible gift. It would be a shame to let it go to waste."

"Like you, you mean?" Shane asked acidly.

"What do you mean?" I shook my head. "I'm not wasting my gift for music. That's one of the reasons I'm here."

"I'm not talking," Shane said, "about your gift for *music*."

I stared at him. His meaning was suddenly clear. *Too* clear. There were still people, of course, standing nearby, watching, listening. Thanks to his theatrics, we'd attracted quite a little crowd. Some of the kids who hadn't made it to the music building yet, and quite a few of the counselors, had gathered around to watch the little drama unfolding in front of the dining hall. They wouldn't, I'm sure, know what he was referring to. But I did. I knew.

"Shane," I said. "That's not fair."

"Yeah?" He snorted. "Well, you know what else isn't fair, Jess? My mom, making me come here. And you, not giving Lionel a strike!"

And with that, he took off without another word.

"Shane," I called after him. "Come back here. I swear, if you don't come back here, it's the porch with Paul Huck for you tonight—"

Shane stopped, but not because I'd intimidated him with my threat. Oh, no. He stopped because he'd run smack into Dr. Alistair, the camp director, who—having apparently heard the commotion from inside the dining hall, where he often sat after all the campers were gone and enjoyed a quiet cup of coffee—had come outside to investigate.

"*Oof,*" Dr. Alistair said, as Shane's mullet head sank into his midriff. He reached down to grasp the boy by the shoulders in an attempt to keep them both from toppling over. Shane was no lightweight, you know.

"What," Dr. Alistair asked, as he steered Shane back around toward me, "is the meaning of all this caterwauling?"

Before I could say a word, Shane lifted his head and, staring up at Dr. Alistair with a face that was perfectly devoid of tears—but upon which there was an unmistakable bruise growing under one eye—said, "A boy hit me and my counselor didn't do anything, Dr. Alistair." He added, with a hiccupy sob, "If my dad finds out about this, he's going to be plenty mad, boy."

Dr. Alistair glared at me from behind the lenses of his glasses. "Is this true, young lady?" he demanded. He only called me young lady, I'm sure, because he couldn't remember my name.

"Only partially," I said. "I mean, another boy did hit him, but only after—"

Before I could finish my explanation, however, Dr. Alistair was taking charge of the situation.

"You," he said to Dave, who'd been standing close by, watching the proceedings with open-mouthed wonder. "Take this boy here to the nurse to have his eye looked at."

Dave sprang to attention. "Yes, sir," he said and, throwing me an apologetic look, he put a hand on Shane's shoulder and began steering him toward the infirmary. "Come on, big guy," he said.

Shane, sniffling, went with him . . . after pausing to throw me a triumphant look.

"You," Dr. Alistair said, jabbing his index finger at me. "You and I are going to meet in my office to discuss this matter."

My ears, I could tell, were redder than ever. "Yes, sir," I murmured. It was only then that I noticed that there among the onlookers stood Karen Sue Hanky, her mouth forming a little *V* of delight. How I longed to ram my fist, as Lionel had his, into her rat face.

"But not," Dr. Alistair continued, pausing to look down at his watch, "until one o'clock. I have a seminar until then."

And without another word, he turned around and headed back into the dining hall.

My shoulders slumped. One o'clock? Well, that was it. I was fired for sure.

Because of course there was no way I was making my meeting with Dr. Alistair. Not when I had an appointment at the same time to check out the situation with Keely Herzberg. I mean, my job was important, I guess. But not as important as a little girl who may or may not have been stolen from her custodial parent.

Remember what I was saying about how complicated my life had gotten lately? Yeah. That about summed it up.

"I told you," Karen Sue said as soon as Dr. Alistair was out of earshot, "that violence is never the answer."

I glanced at her sourly. "Hey, Karen Sue," I said.

She looked at me warily. "What?"

I made a gesture with my finger that caused her to gasp and go stalking off.

I noticed that a lot of the other counselors who were still standing there seemed to find it quite amusing, however.

CHAPTER

10

He was late.

I stood on the side of the road, trying not to notice the sweat that was prickling the back of my neck. Not just the back of my neck, either. There was a pool of it between my boobs. I'm serious.

And I wasn't too comfortable in my jeans, either.

But what choice did I have? I'd learned the hard way never to ride a motorcycle in shorts. The scar was gone, but not the memory of the way the skin of my calf, sizzling against the exhaust pipe, had smelled.

Still, it had to be a hundred degrees on that long, narrow road. There were plenty of trees, of course, to offer shade. Hell, Camp Wawasee was nothing but trees, except where it was lake.

But if I stood in the trees, Rob might not see me when he came roaring up, and he might whiz right on past, and precious moments might be lost. . . .

Not that it mattered. I was going to be fired any-way, on account of missing my one o'clock meeting with Dr. Alistair. I was willing to bet that by the time I got back, all my stuff would be packed up and wait-ing for me by the front gates. Kerplunk, she sunk, like junk, cha, cha, cha.

Sweat was beginning to drip from the crown of my head, beneath my hair and into my eyes, when I finally heard the far off sound of a motorcycle engine. Rob isn't the type to let a muffler go, so his Indian didn't have one of those annoyingly loud engines you can hear from miles away. I simply became aware of a sound other than the shrill whine of the cicadas that were in the tall grass along the side of the road, and then I saw him, clipping along at no mean pace.

I didn't have to—we were the only two people on the road for miles, Lake Wawasee being about as iso-lated, I was becoming convinced, as Ice Station Zebra—but I put my arm out, to make sure he saw me. I mean, he could have thought I was a mirage or something. It was one of those kind of blazingly hot sunny days when you looked down a long straight road and saw pools of water across it, even though, when you finally got to the pool, it had evaporated as if it had never been there . . . because, of course, it hadn't been. It had just been one of those optical illu-sions they talk about, you know, in human bio.

Rob came cruising up to me and then put out a booted foot to balance himself when he came to a stop. He looked, as always, impressively large, like a lumberjack or something, only more stylishly dressed.

And when he took off his helmet and squinted at me in the sunlight with those eyes—so pale blue, they were practically the same color gray as his bike's exhaust—and I drank in his sexily messed-up hair and his darkly tanned forearms, all I could think was that, bad as it had been, that whole thing with the lightning and Colonel Jenkins and all, it had actually been worth it, because it had brought me the hottest Hottie of them all, Rob.

Well, sort of, anyway.

"Hey, sailor," I said. "Give a girl a ride?"

Rob just gave me his trademark don't-mess-with-me frown, then popped open the box on the back of his bike where he keeps the spare helmet.

"Get on," was all he said, as he held the helmet out to me.

Like I needed an invitation. I snatched up the helmet, jammed it into place (trying not to think about my sweaty hair), then wrapped my arms around his waist and said, "Put the pedal to the metal, dude."

He gave me one last, half-disgusted, half-amused look, then put his own helmet back on.

And we were off.

Hey, it wasn't a big, wet one or anything, but "Get on" isn't bad. I mean, Rob may not be completely in love with me yet or anything, but he'd shown up, right? That had to count for something. I mean, I'd called him that morning, and said I needed him to drive for four hours, cross-country, to pick me up.

And he'd shown up. He'd have had to find someone to cover for him at work, and explain to his uncle why he couldn't be there. He'd have had to buy gas, both for the trip to Chicago and then back again. He'd be spending a total of ten hours or so on the road. Tomorrow, he'd probably be exhausted.

But he'd shown up.

And I didn't think he was doing it because it was such a worthy cause, either. I mean, it *was*, and all, but he wasn't doing it for Keely.

At least . . . God, I *hope* not.

By two-thirty, we were cruising along Lake Shore Drive. The city looked bright and clean, the windows of the skyscrapers sparkling in the sunlight. The beaches were crowded. The songs playing from the car radios of the traffic we passed made it seem like we were a couple in a music video, or on a TV commercial or something. For Levi's, maybe. I mean, here we were, two total Hotties—well, okay, one total Hottie. I'm probably only Do-able—tooling around on the back of a completely cherried-out Indian on a sunny summer day. How much cooler could you get?

I guess if we'd noticed from the beginning we were being followed, that might have been cooler. But we didn't.

I didn't because I was busy experiencing one of those epiphanies they always talk about in English class.

Only my epiphany, instead of being some kind of spiritual enlightenment or whatever, was just this gush of total happiness because I had my arms around this totally buff guy I'd had a crush on since what seemed like forever, and he smelled really good, like Coast deodorant soap and whatever laundry detergent his mother uses on his T-shirts, and he had to think that I was at least somewhat cute, or he wouldn't have come all that way to pick me up. I was thinking, if only this was how I could spend the rest of my life: riding around the country on the back of Rob's bike, listening to music out of other people's car radios, and maybe stopping every once in a while for some nachos or whatever.

I don't know what was occupying Rob's thoughts so much that he didn't see the white van on our tail. Maybe he was having an epiphany of his own. Hey, it could happen.

But anyway, what happened was, eventually we had to pull off Lake Shore Drive in order to get where Keely was, and little by little, the traffic thinned out, and we still didn't notice the van purring along behind us. I don't know for sure, of course, because we weren't paying attention, but I like to think it stayed at least a couple car lengths away. Otherwise, well, there's no other explanation for it. We're just idiots. Or at least I am.

Anyway, finally we pulled onto this tree-lined street that was one hundred percent residential. I knew exactly which one Keely was in, of course, but I made Rob park about three houses away, just to be on the safe side. I mean, *that* much I knew. *That* much I was paying attention to.

We stood in front of the place where Keely was staying. It was just a house. A city house, so it was kind of narrow. On one side of it ran a skinny alley. The other side was attached to the house next door. Keely's house hadn't been painted as recently as the one next to it. What paint was left on it was kind of peeling off in a sad way. I would call the neighborhood sketchy, at best. The small yards had an untended look to them. Grass grows fast in a humid climate like the one in northern Illinois, and needs constant attention. No one on this street seemed to care, particularly, how high their grass grew, or what kind of garbage lay in their yards for that grass to swallow.

Maybe that was the purpose of the high grass. To hide the garbage.

Rob, standing next to me as I gazed up at the house, said, "Nice-looking crack den."

I winced. "It's not that bad," I said.

"Yeah, it is," he said.

"Well." I squared my shoulders. I wasn't sweaty anymore, after having so much wind blown on me, but I soon would be, if I stood on that hot sidewalk much longer. "Here goes nothing."

I opened the gate in the low chain-link fence that surrounded the house, and strode up the cement steps to the front door. I didn't realize Rob had followed me until I'd reached out to ring the bell.

"So what exactly," he said, as we listened to the hollow ringing deep inside the house, "is the plan here?"

I said, "There's no plan."

"Great." Rob's expression didn't change. "My favorite kind."

"Who is it?" demanded a woman's voice from behind the closed door. She didn't sound very happy about having been disturbed.

"Hello, ma'am?" I called. "Hi, my name is Ginger Silverman, and this is my friend, Nate. We're seniors at Chicago Central High School, and we're doing a research project on parental attitudes toward children's television programming. We were wondering if we could ask you a few questions about the kinds of television programs your children like to watch. It will only take a minute, and will be of invaluable help to us."

Rob looked at me like I was insane. "Ginger Silverman?"

I shrugged. "I like that name."

He shook his head. "*Nate?*"

"I like that name, too."

Inside the house, locks were being undone. When the door was thrown back, I saw, through the screen door, a tall, skinny woman in cutoffs and a halter top. You could tell she'd once taken care to color her hair, but that that had sort of fallen by the wayside. Now the ends of her hair were blonde, but the two inches of it at the top were dark brown. On her forehead, not quite hidden by her two-tone hair, was a dark, crescent-moon-shaped scab, about an inch and a half long. Out of one corner of her mouth, which was as flat and skinny as the rest of her, dangled a cigarette.

She looked at Rob and me as if we had dropped down from another planet and asked her to join the Galaxian Federation, or something.

"What?" she said.

I repeated my spiel about Chicago Central High School—who even knew if there was such a place?—and our thesis on children's television programming. As I spoke, a small child appeared from the shadows behind Mrs. Herzberg—if, indeed, this was Mrs. Herzberg, though I suspected it was—and, wrapping her arms around the woman's leg, blinked up at us with big brown eyes.

I recognized her instantly. Keely Herzberg.

"Mommy," Keely said curiously, "who are they?"

"Just some kids," Mrs. Herzberg said. She took her cigarette out of her mouth and I noticed that her fingernails were very bleedy-looking. "Look," she said to us. "We aren't interested. Okay?"

She was starting to close the door when I added, "There's a ten-dollar remuneration to all participants. . . ."

The door instantly froze. Then it swung open again.

"Ten bucks?" Mrs. Herzberg said. Her tired eyes, under that crescent-shaped scab, looked suddenly brighter.

"Uh-huh," I said. "In cash. Just for answering a few questions."

Mrs. Herzberg shrugged her skinny shoulders, and then, exhaling a plume of blue smoke at us through the screen door, she went, "Shoot."

"Okay," I said eagerly. "Um, what's your daughter's—this is your daughter, isn't it?"

The woman nodded without looking down. "Yeah."

"Okay. What is your daughter's favorite television show?"

"*Sesame Street*," said Mrs. Herzberg, while her daughter said, "*Rugrats*," at the same time.

"No, Mommy," Keely said, tugging on her mother's shorts. "*Rugrats*."

"*Sesame Street*," Mrs. Herzberg said. "My daughter is only allowed to watch public television."

Keely shrieked, "*Rugrats!*"

Mrs. Herzberg looked down at her daughter and said, "If you don't quit it, I'm sending you out back to play."

Keely's lower lip was trembling. "But you know I like *Rugrats* best, Mommy."

"Sweetheart," Mrs. Herzberg said. "Mommy is trying to answer these people's questions. Please do not interrupt."

"Um," I said. "Maybe we should move on. Do you and your husband discuss with one another the kinds of television shows your daughter is allowed to watch?"

"No," Mrs. Herzberg said shortly. "And I don't let her watch junk, like that *Rugrats*."

"But, Mommy," Keely said, her eyes filled with tears, "I love them."

"That's it," Mrs. Herzberg said. She pointed with her cigarette toward the back of the house. "Outside. Now."

"But, Mommy—"

"No," Mrs. Herzberg said. "That's it. I told you once. Now go outside and play, and let Mommy talk to these people."

Keely, letting out a hiccuppy little sob, disappeared. I heard a screen door slam somewhere in the house.

"Go on," Mrs. Herzberg said to me. Then her eyebrows knit. "Shouldn't you be writing my answers down?"

I reached up to smack myself on the forehead. "The clipboard!" I said to Rob. "I forgot the clipboard!"

"Well," Rob says. "Then I guess that's the end of that. Sorry to trouble you, ma'am—"

"No," I said, grabbing him by the arm and steering him closer to the screen door. "That's okay. It's in the car. I'll just go get it. You keep asking questions while I *go and get the clipboard.*"

Rob's pale blue eyes, as he looked down at me, definitely had ice chips in them, but what was I supposed to do? I went, "Ask her about the kind of programming *she* likes, Nate. And don't forget the ten bucks," and then I bounded down the steps, through the overgrown yard, out the gate . . .

And then, when I was sure Rob had Mrs. Herzberg distracted, I darted down the alley alongside her house, until I came to a high wooden fence that separated her backyard from the street.

It only took me a minute to climb up onto a Dumpster that was sitting there, and then look over that fence into the backyard.

Keely was there. She was sitting in one of those green plastic turtles people fill with sand. In her hand was a very dirty, very naked Barbie doll. She was singing softly to it.

Perfect, I thought. If Rob could just keep Mrs. Herzberg busy for a few minutes . . .

I clambered over the fence, then dropped over the other side into Keely's yard. Somehow, in spite of my gymnast-like grace and James Bondian stealthiness, Keely heard me, and squinted at me through the strong sunlight.

"Hey," I said as I ambled over to her sandbox. "What's up?"

Keely stared at me with those enormous brown eyes. "You aren't supposed to be back here," she informed me gravely.

"Yeah," I said, sitting down on the edge of the sandbox beside her. I'd have sat in the grass, but like in the front yard, it was long and straggly-looking, and after my recent tick experience, I wasn't too anxious to encounter any more bloodsucking parasites.

"I know I'm not supposed to be back here," I said to Keely. "But I wanted to ask you a couple of questions. Is that okay?"

Keely shrugged and looked down at her doll. "I guess," she said.

I looked down at the doll, too. "What happened to Barbie's clothes?"

"She lost them," Keely said.

"Whoa," I said. "Too bad. Think your mom will buy her some more?"

Keely shrugged again, and began dipping Barbie's head into the sandbox, stirring the sand like it was cake batter, and Barbie was a mixer. The sand in the sandbox didn't smell too fresh, if you know what I mean. I had a feeling some of the neighborhood cats had been there a few times.

"What about your dad?" I asked her. "Could your dad buy you some more Barbie clothes?"

Keely said, lifting Barbie from the sand and then smoothing her hair back, "My daddy's in heaven."

Well. That settled that, didn't it?

"Who told you that your daddy is in heaven, Keely?" I asked her.

Keely shrugged, her gaze riveted to the plastic doll in her hands. "My mommy," she said. Then she added, "I have a new daddy now." She wrenched her gaze from the Barbie and looked up at me, her dark eyes huge. "But I don't like him as much as my old daddy."

My mouth had gone dry . . . as dry as the sand beneath our feet. Somehow I managed to croak, "Really? Why not?"

Keely shrugged and looked away from me again. "He throws things," she said. "He threw a bottle, and it hit my mommy in the head, and blood came out, and she started crying."

I thought about the crescent-shaped scab on Mrs. Herzberg's forehead. It was exactly the size and shape a bottle, flying at a high velocity, would make.

And that, I knew, was that.

I guess I could have gotten out of there, called the

cops, and let them handle it. But did I really want to put the poor kid through all that? Armed men knocking her mother's door down, guns drawn, and all of that? Who knew what the mother's bottle-throwing boyfriend was like? Maybe he'd try to shoot it out with the cops. Innocent people might get hurt. You don't know. You can't predict these things. I know *I* can't, and I'm the one with the psychic powers.

And yeah, Keely's mother seemed like kind of a freak, protesting that her kid only watches public television while standing there filling that same kid's lungs with carcinogens. But hey, there are worse things a parent could do. That didn't make her an unfit mother. I mean, it wasn't like she was taking that cigarette and putting it out on Keely's arm, like some parents I've seen on the news.

But telling the kid her father was dead? And shacking up with a guy who throws bottles?

Not so nice.

So even though I felt like a complete jerk about it, I knew what I had to do.

I think you'd have done the same thing, too, in my place. I mean, really, what else could anybody have done?

I stood up and said, "Keely, your dad's not in heaven. If you come with me right now, I'll take you to him."

Keely had to crane her neck to look up at me. The sun was so bright, she had to do some pretty serious squinting, too.

"My daddy's not in heaven?" she asked. "Where is he, then?"

That was when I heard it: the sound of Rob's motorcycle engine. I could tell the sound of that bike's engine from every single other motorcycle in my entire town.

I know it's stupid. It's more than stupid. It's pathetic, is what it is. But can you really blame me? I mean, I really did harbor this hope that Rob was pining for me, and satisfied his carnal longing for me by riding by my house late at night.

He never actually did this, but my ears had become so accustomed to straining for the sound of his bike's engine, I could have picked it out in a traffic jam.

The real question, of course, was why Rob had left Mrs. Herzberg's front porch when he had to know I wasn't finished with my business in her backyard.

Something was wrong. Something was very wrong.

Which was why I didn't suffer too much twinging of my conscience when I looked down at Keely and said, "Your daddy's at McDonald's. If we hurry, we can catch him there, and he'll buy you a Happy Meal."

Did I feel bad, invoking the *M* word in order to lure a kid out of her own backyard? Sure. I felt like a worm. Worse than a worm. I felt like I was Karen Sue Hanky, or someone equally as creepy.

But I also felt like I had no other choice. Rob's bike roaring to life just then meant one thing, and one thing only:

We had to get going. And now.

It worked. Thank God, it worked. Because Keely Herzberg, bless her five-year-old heart, stood up and, looking up into my face, shrugged and said, "Okay."

It was at that moment I realized why Rob had taken off. The screen door that led to the backyard burst open, and a man in a pair of fairly tight-fitting jeans and some heavy-looking work boots—and who was clutching a beer bottle—came out onto the back porch and roared, "Who the hell are you?"

I grabbed Keely by the hand. I knew, of course, who this was. And I could only pray that his aim, when it came to moving targets, left something to be desired.

The sound of Rob's motorcycle engine had been getting closer. I knew now what he was doing.

"Come on," I said to Keely.

And then we were running.

I didn't really think about what I was doing. If I had stopped and thought about it, of course, I would have been able to see that there was no way that we could run faster than Mrs. Herzberg's boyfriend. All he had to do was leap down from the back porch and he'd be on us.

Fortunately, I was too scared of getting whacked with a beer bottle to do much thinking.

Instead, what I did was, while we ran, I shifted my grip on Keely from her hand to her arm, until I had scooped her up in both hands and she was being swept through the air. And when we reached the part of the fence I'd jumped down from, I swung her, with all my strength, toward the top of the fence. . . .

And she went sailing over it, just like those sacks of produce Professor Le Blanc had predicted I was going to be spending the rest of my life bagging.

Professor Le Blanc was right. I was a bag girl, in a way. Only what I bagged wasn't groceries, but other people's mistreated kids.

I heard Keely land with a scrape of plastic sandals on metal. She had made it onto the lid of the Dumpster, where, I could only hope, Rob would grab her. Now it was my turn.

Only Keely's new bottle-throwing dad was right behind me. He had let out a shocked, *"Hey!"* when I'd thrown Keely over the fence. The next thing I knew, the ground was shaking—I swear I felt it shudder beneath my feet—as he leaped from the porch and thundered toward me. Behind us a screen door banged open, and I heard Mrs. Herzberg yell, "Clay! Where's Keely, Clay?"

"Not me," I heard Clay grunt. *"Her!"*

That was it. I was dead.

But I wasn't giving up. Not until that bottle was beating my skull into pulp. Instead, I jumped, grabbing for the top of the fence.

I got it, but not without incurring some splinters. I didn't care about my hands, though. I was halfway there. All I had to do was swing my leg over, and—

He had hold of my foot. My left foot. He had grabbed it, and was trying to drag me down.

"Oh, no, you don't, girlie," Clay growled at me.

With his other hand, he grabbed the back of my jeans. He had apparently dropped the beer bottle, with was something of a relief.

Except that in a second, he was going to lift me off that fence, throw me to the ground, and step on me with one of those giant, work-booted feet.

"Jess!" I heard Rob calling to me. "Jess, come *on!*"

Oh, okay. I'll just hurry up now. Sorry about the delay, I'm just putting on a little lipstick—

"You," Clay said, as he tugged on me, "are in big trouble, girlie—"

Which was when I launched my free foot in the direction of his face. It connected solidly with the bridge of his nose, making a crunching sound that was quite satisfying, to my ears.

Well, I've never liked being called girlie.

Clay let go of both my foot and my waistband with an outraged cry of pain. And the second I was free, I swung myself over that fence, landed with a thump on the roof of the Dumpster, then jumped straight from the Dumpster onto the back of Rob's bike, which was waiting beneath it.

"Go!" I shrieked, throwing my arms around him and Keely, who was huddled, wide-eyed, on the seat in front of him.

Rob didn't waste another second. He didn't sit around and argue about how neither Keely nor I were wearing helmets, or how I'd probably ruined his shocks, jumping from the Dumpster onto his bike, like a cowboy onto the back of a horse.

Instead, he lifted up his foot and we were off, tearing down that alley like something NASA had launched.

Even with the noise of Rob's engine, I could still hear the anguished shriek behind us.

"Keely!"

It was Mrs. Herzberg. She didn't know it, of course, but I wasn't stealing her daughter. I was saving her.

But as for Keely's mother . . .

Well, she was a grown-up. She was just going to have to save herself.

CHAPTER

11

I don't know what your feelings on McDonald's are. I mean, I know McDonald's is at least partly responsible for the destruction of the South American rain forest, which they have apparently razed large sections of in order to make grazing pastures for all the cattle they need to slaughter each year in order to make enough Big Macs to satisfy the demand, and all.

And I know that there's been some criticism over the fact that every seven miles, in America, there is at least one McDonald's. Not a hospital, mind you, or a police station, but a McDonald's, every seven miles.

I mean, that's sort of scary, if you think about it.

On the other hand, if you've been going to McDonald's since you were a little kid, like most of us have, it's sort of comforting to see those golden arches. I mean, they represent something more than just high-fat, high-cholesterol fast food. They mean that wherever you are, well, you're actually not that far from home.

And those fries are killer.

Fortunately, there was a Mickey D's just a few blocks away from Keely's house. Thank God, or I think Rob would have had an embolism. I could tell Rob was pretty unhappy about having to transport Keely and me, both helmetless, on the back of his Indian . . . even though it was completely safe, with me holding onto her and all. And it wasn't like he ever went more than fifteen miles per hour the whole time.

Well, except when we'd been racing down that alley to get away from Clay.

But let me tell you, when we pulled into the parking lot of that McDonald's, I could tell Rob was plenty relieved.

And when we stepped into the icy air-conditioning, *I* was relieved. I was sweating like a pig. I don't mind the crime-fighting stuff so much. It's the humidity that bugs me.

Anyway, once we were inside, and Keely was enjoying her Happy Meal while I thirstily sucked down a Coke, Rob explained how he'd been listening attentively to Mrs. Herzberg's description of her television-viewing habits, when her boyfriend appeared as if from nowhere, preemptively ending their little interview with a fist against the door frame. Sensing trouble, Rob hastily excused himself—though he did fork over the promised ten-dollar bill—and came looking for me.

Thank God he had, too, or I'd be the one with a footprint across my face, as opposed to Clay.

I tried to pay him back the ten he'd given to Mrs. Herzberg. He wouldn't take my money though. Also, he insisted on paying for Keely's Happy Meal and my giant Coke. I let him, thinking if I were lucky, he might expect me to put out for it.

Ha. I wish.

Then, once we'd compared notes on our adventures with Clay, I left Rob sitting with Keely while I got on the pay phone and dialed Jonathan Herzberg's office.

A woman answered. She said Mr. Herzberg couldn't come to the phone right now, on account of being in a meeting.

I said, "Well, tell him to get out of it. I have his kid here, and I don't know what I'm supposed to do with her."

I didn't realize until after the woman had put me on hold that I'd probably sounded like a kidnapper, or something. I wondered if she was running around the office, telling the other secretaries to call the police and have the call traced or something.

But I doubt she had time. Mr. Herzberg picked up again almost right away.

"Hey," I said. "It's me, Jess. I'm at a McDonald's—" I gave him the address. "I have Keely here. Can you come pick her up? I'd bring her to you, but we're on a motorcycle."

"Fifteen m-minutes." Mr. Herzberg was stammering with excitement.

"Good." I started to hang up, but I heard him say something else. I brought the phone back to my ear. "What was that?"

"God bless you," Mr. Herzberg said. He sounded kind of choked up.

"Uh," I said. "Yeah. Okay. Just hurry."

I hung up. I guess that's the only good part about this whole thing. You know, that sometimes, I can reunite kids with the parents who love them.

Still, I wish they didn't have to get so mushy about it.

It was after I'd hung up and felt around in the change dispenser to see if anybody had left anything behind—hey, you never know—that I noticed the van.

I walked over to where Rob and Keely were sitting.

"Hey," I said. "We got visitors."

Rob looked around the restaurant. "Oh, yeah?"

"Outside," I said. "The white van. Don't look. I'll take care of it. You stay here with Keely."

Rob shrugged, and dipped a fry into some ketchup. "No problem," he said.

To Keely, I said, "Your dad's on his way."

Keely grinned happily and sucked on the straw in her milk shake.

I went up to the counter and ordered two cheeseburger meals to go. Then I took the two bags and the little cardboard drink holder and went out the door opposite the one where the van was sitting. Then I walked all the way around the outside of the restaurant, past the drive-through window and the Dumpsters out back, until I came up behind the van.

Then I opened the side door and climbed on in.

"Ooh," I said appreciatively. "Nice air you got in here. But you'll wear out the battery if you sit here and idle for too long."

Special Agents Johnson and Smith turned around and looked at me. They both had sunglasses on. Special Agent Smith lifted hers up and looked at me with her pretty blue eyes.

"Hi, Jessica," she said, in a resigned sort of way.

"Hi," I said. "I figured you guys might be getting hungry, so I brought you this." I passed her the drinks and the bags with the cheeseburgers and fries in them. "I super-sized it for you."

Special Agent Smith opened her bag and looked inside it. "Thanks, Jess," she said, sounding pleasantly surprised. "That was very thoughtful."

"Yes," Special Agent Johnson said. "Thank you, Jessica."

But he said it in this certain way that you could just tell he was kind of, you know. Unhappy.

"So how long have you guys been following me?" I asked.

Special Agent Johnson—who hadn't even touched his food—said, "Since shortly after you left the camp."

"Really?" I thought about this. "All the way from there? I didn't notice you."

"We *are* professionals," Special Agent Smith pointed out, nibbling on a fry.

"We're *supposed* to be, anyway," Special Agent

Johnson said, in this meaningful way that made his partner put down the fry she was eating and look guilty. "How'd you know we were here, anyway?" he asked me.

"Come on," I said. "There's been a white van sitting on my street back home for months now. You think I wouldn't notice?"

"Ah," Special Agent Johnson said.

We sat there, all three of us, basking in the air-conditioning and inhaling the delicious scent of fries. There was a lot of stuff in the back of the van, stuff with blinking red and green buttons. It looked like surveillance equipment to me, but I could have been wrong. Nice to know the government wasn't wasting the taxpayers' money on frivolous things like the monitoring of teen psychics.

Finally, the luscious odor of Mickey D's proved too much for Special Agent Smith. She reached into her bag again and this time pulled out one of the cheeseburgers, then began unwrapping it. When she noticed Special Agent Johnson glaring at her disapprovingly, she went, "Well, it's just going to get cold, Allan," and took a big bite.

"So," I said. "How you two been?"

"Fine," Special Agent Smith said, with her mouth full.

"We're doing all right," Special Agent Johnson said. "We'd like to talk to you, though."

"If you wanted to talk to me," I said, "you could have just stopped by. I mean, you obviously know where to find me."

"Who's the little girl?" Special Agent Johnson said, nodding toward the window, where Rob and Keely were sitting.

"Oh, her?" I leaned forward and, since he obviously didn't want them, dug my hand into Special Agent Johnson's fries and pulled out a bunch for myself. "She's my cousin," I said.

"You don't have any cousins that age," Special Agent Smith said, after taking a sip from the soda I'd bought her.

"I don't?"

"No," she said. "You don't."

"Well," I said. "She's Rob's cousin, then."

"Really?" Special Agent Johnson took out a notepad and a pen. "And what's Rob's last name?"

"Ha," I said, with my mouth full of fry. "Like I'd tell you."

"He's kind of cute," Special Agent Smith observed.

"I know," I said, with a sigh.

The sigh must have been telling, since Special Agent Smith went, "Is he your boyfriend?"

"Not yet," I said. "But he will be."

"Really? When?"

"When I turn eighteen. Or when he is no longer able to resist the overwhelming attraction he feels for me and jumps my bones. Whichever comes first."

Special Agent Smith burst out laughing. Her partner didn't look so amused though.

"Jessica," he said. "Would you like to tell us about Taylor Monroe?"

I cocked my head innocently to one side. "Who?"

"Taylor Monroe," Special Agent Johnson said. "Disappeared two years ago. An anonymous call was placed yesterday to 1-800-WHERE-R-YOU, giving an address in Gainesville, Florida, where the boy could be found."

"Oh, yeah?" I picked at a loose thread on my jeans. "And was he there?"

"He was." Special Agent Johnson's gaze, reflected in the rearview mirror, did not waver from mine. "You wouldn't know anything about that, would you, Jess?"

"Me?" I screwed up my face. "No way. That's great, though. His parents must be pretty happy, huh?"

"They're ecstatic," Special Agent Smith said, taking a sip from her Coke. "The couple who took him—they apparently couldn't have children of their own—are in jail, and Taylor's already been returned to his folks. You never saw a more joyous reunion."

"Aw," I said, genuinely pleased. "That's sweet."

Special Agent Johnson adjusted the rearview mirror so he could see my reflection more clearly. "Very nicely done," he said drily. "I almost believed you had nothing to do with it."

"Well," I said. "I didn't."

"Jessica." Special Agent Johnson shook his head. "When are you finally going to admit that you lied to us last spring?"

"I don't know," I said. "Maybe when you admit

that you made a big mistake marrying Mrs. Johnson and that your heart really belongs to Jill here."

Special Agent Smith choked on a mouthful of cheeseburger. Special Agent Johnson had to ram her on the back a couple of times before she could breathe again.

"Oh," I said. "That go down the wrong pipe? I hate when that happens."

"Jessica." Special Agent Johnson spun around in his seat—well, as much as he could with the steering wheel in the way—and eyed me wrathfully. Really. *Wrathful* is about the only way I can describe it. Hey, I took the PSATs. I know what I'm talking about.

"You may think you got away with something last spring," he growled, "with that whole going-to-the-press thing. But I am warning you, missy. We are on to you. We know what you've been up to. And it's just a matter of time—"

Over Special Agent Johnson's shoulder, I saw a Passat come barreling through the intersection. Brakes squealing, it pulled into the McDonald's parking lot and came to a stop a few spaces down from the van. Jonathan Herzberg popped out from the driver's seat, so anxious to see his daughter he forgot to take off his seat belt. It strangled him, and he had to sit back down and unsnap it before he could get up again.

"—before Jill or I or someone catches you at it, and—"

"And what?" I asked. "What are you going to do to me, Allan? Put me in jail? For what? I haven't done anything illegal. Just because I won't help you find your little murderers and your drug lords and your escaped convicts, you think I'm doing something wrong? Well, excuse me for not wanting to do your job for you."

Special Agent Smith laid a hand on her partner's shoulder. "Allan," she said, in a warning voice.

Special Agent Johnson just kept glaring at me. He'd been so upset, he'd knocked over his fries, and now they lay all over the floor beneath his feet. He had already squashed one into the blue carpeting beneath the gas pedal. Behind him, Jonathan Herzberg was hurrying into the restaurant, having already spotted his daughter through the window.

"One thing you can do for me, though," I said, amiably enough. "You can tell me who tipped you off that I'd left the campgrounds."

I saw them exchange glances.

"Tipped us off?" Special Agent Smith ran her fingertips through her light brown hair, which was cut into a stylish—but not too stylish—bob. "What are you talking about, Jess?"

"Oh, what?" I rolled my eyes. "You expect me to believe the two of you have been sitting in this van outside of Camp Wawasee for the past nine days, waiting to see when I'd leave? I don't think so. For one thing, there aren't nearly enough food wrappers on the floor."

"Jessica," Special Agent Smith said, "we haven't been spying on you."

"No," I said. "You've just been paying somebody else to do it."

"Jess—"

"Don't bother to deny it. How else would you have known I was leaving the camp?" I shook my head. "Who is it, anyway? Pamela? That secretary who looks like John Wayne? Oh, wait, I know." I snapped my fingers. "It's Karen Sue Hanky, isn't it? No, wait, she's too much of a crybaby to be a narc."

"You," Special Agent Johnson said, "are being ridiculous."

Ridiculous. Yeah. That's right.

I watched through the plate glass window as Jonathan Herzberg snatched up his daughter and gave her a hug that came close to strangling her. She didn't seem to mind, though. Her grin was broader than I'd ever seen it—way bigger than it had been over the Happy Meal.

Another joyous reunion, brought about by me.

And I was missing it.

Ridiculous. They were the ones going around spying on a sixteen-year-old girl. And they said *I* was being ridiculous.

"Well," I said. "It's been fun, you guys, but I gotta motor. Bye."

I got out of the van. Behind me, I heard Special Agent Johnson call my name.

But I didn't bother turning around.

I don't like being called missy any more than I liked being called girlie. I was proud that I'd at least managed to restrain myself from slamming my foot into Special Agent Johnson's face.

Mr. Goodhart was really going to be pleased by the progress I'd made so far this summer.

CHAPTER

12

"So," Rob said. "Was it worth it?"

"I don't know," I said with a shrug. "I mean, her mom didn't seem that bad. She might have gotten out on her own, eventually."

"Yeah," Rob said. "After enough stitches."

I didn't say anything. Rob was the one who came from the broken home, not me. I figured he knew what he was talking about.

"She claims her favorite TV show is *Masterpiece Theater*," Rob informed me.

"Well," I said. "That doesn't prove anything. Except, you know, that she wanted to impress us."

"Impress Ginger and Nate," he said, with one raised eyebrow, "from Chicago Central High? Yeah, that's important."

"Well," I said. I rested my elbows on my knees. We were sitting on a picnic table, gazing out over

Lake Wawasee. Well, the edge of Lake Wawasee, anyway. We were about two miles from the actual camp. Somehow, I just couldn't bring myself to go back there. Maybe it was the fact that when I set foot through those gates, I was going to be fired.

Then again, maybe it was because when I set foot through those gates, I'd have to say good-bye to Rob.

Look, I'll admit it: I'm warm for the guy's form. Anybody here have a problem with that?

And it was really nice, sitting there in the shade with him, listening to the shrill *whirr* of the cicadas and the birdsong from the treetops. It seemed as if there wasn't another human being for miles and miles. Above the trees, clouds were gathering. Soon it was going to rain, but it looked as if it would hold off for a little while longer—besides, we were somewhat protected by the canopy of leaves over our heads.

If it had been dark enough, it would have been a perfect make-out spot.

Well, if Rob didn't have this total prejudice against making out with girls sixteen and under.

It was as I was sadly counting the months until I turned seventeen—all eight and a half of them; Douglas could have told me exactly how many days, and even minutes, I had left—that Rob reached out and put his arm around me.

And unlike when Pamela had done the exact same thing, I did not mind. I did not mind at all.

"Hey," Rob said. I could feel his heart thudding against my side, where his chest pressed against me.

"Stop beating yourself up. You did the right thing. You always do."

For a minute, I couldn't figure out what he was talking about. Then I remembered. Oh, yeah. Keely Herzberg. Rob thought I'd been mulling over her, when really, I'd just been trying to figure out a way to get him to make a pass at me.

Oh, well. I figured what I was doing was working so far, if the arm around me was any indication. I sighed and tried to look sad . . . which was difficult, because I was sort of having another one of those epiphanies, what with the breeze off the lake and the birds and Rob's Coast deodorant soap smell and the nice, heavy weight of his arm and everything.

"I guess," I said, managing to sound uncertain even to my own ears.

"Are you kidding?" Rob gave me a friendly squeeze. "That woman told her kid that her father was dead. *Dead!* You think she was playing with a full deck?"

"I know," I said. Maybe if I looked sad enough, he'd stick his tongue in my mouth.

"And look how happy Keely was. And Mr. Herzberg. My God, did you see how stoked he was to have his kid back? I think if you'd have let him, he'd have written you a check for five grand, right there and then."

Jonathan Herzberg had been somewhat eager to offer me compensation for the trouble I'd taken, returning his daughter to him . . . a substantial monetary reward I had politely turned down, telling him that if he absolutely had to fork his money over to somebody, he should donate it to 1-800-WHERE-R-YOU.

Because, I mean, let's face it: you can't go around taking rewards for being human, now can you?

Even if it does get you fired.

"I guess," I said again, still sounding all sad.

But if I'd thought Rob was going to fall for my whole poor-little-me routine, it turned out I had another think coming.

"You can forget it, Mastriani," he said, suddenly removing his arm. "I'm not going to kiss you."

Jeez! What's a girl have to do around here to get felt up?

"Why not?" I demanded.

"We've been over this before," he said, looking bored.

This was true.

"You *used* to kiss me," I pointed out to him.

"That was before I knew you were jailbait."

This was also true.

Rob leaned back, propping himself up on his elbows and gazing out at the trees across the water. In a month or two, all the green leaves he was looking at now would be blazing red and orange. I would be starting my junior year at Ernest Pyle High School, and Rob would still be working in his uncle's garage, helping his mother with the mortgage on their farmhouse (his father had split, as Rob put it, when he was just a little kid, and hadn't been heard from since), and fiddling around with the Harley he was rebuilding in their barn.

But really, if you thought about it, we weren't so different, Rob and I. We both liked going fast, and we both hated liars. Our clothing ensemble of preference was jeans and a T-shirt, and we both had short dark hair . . . mine was even shorter than Rob's. We both loved motorcycles, and neither of us had aspirations for college. At least, I didn't think I did. And I know my grades didn't exactly leave a whole lot of hope for it.

Our similarities completely outweighed our differences. So what if Rob has no curfew, and I have to be home every night by eleven? So what if Rob has a probation officer, and I have a mother who makes me dresses for homecoming dances I'll never go to? People really shouldn't let those things get in the way of true love.

I pointed this out to him, but he didn't look very impressed.

"Look." I flopped down on top of the picnic table, turned toward him on one elbow, holding my head in one hand. "I don't see what the problem is. I mean, I'm going to be seventeen in eight and a half months. Eight and a half months! That's nothing. I don't see why we can't—"

I was lying in just such a way that Rob's face was only a couple of inches from mine. When he turned to look at me, our noses almost bumped into one another.

"Didn't your mother ever tell you," Rob asked, "that you're supposed to play hard to get?"

I looked at his lips. I probably don't need to tell you that they're really nice lips, kind of full and strong-looking. "What," I wanted to know, "is *that* going to get me?"

I swear to you, he was a second away from kissing me then.

I know he said he wasn't going to. But let's face it, he always says that, and then he always does—well, almost always, anyway. I swear that's why he avoids me half the time . . . because he knows that for all he says he isn't going to kiss me, he usually ends up doing it anyway. Who knows why? I'd like to think it's because I'm so damned irresistible, and because he's secretly in love with me, in spite of what it says in the *Cosmo* quiz.

But I wasn't destined to find out. Not just then, anyway. Because just as he was leaning over in the direction of my mouth, this unearthly siren started to wail . . .

. . . and we were both so startled, we wrenched apart.

I swear I thought a tornado alarm was going off. Rob said later he thought it was my dad, with one of those klaxon things old ladies set off when a mugger is attacking them.

But it wasn't either of those things. It was a Wawasee County police cruiser. And it whizzed by the campground we were parked at like a bullet. . . .

Only to be followed by another.

And another.

And then another.

Four squad cars, all headed at breakneck speed in the direction of Camp Wawasee.

I should have known, of course. I should have guessed what was wrong.

But my psychic abilities are limited to finding people, not predicting the future. All I knew was that something was definitely wrong back at the camp . . . and it wasn't my psychic powers telling me that, either. It was just plain common sense.

"What," Rob wanted to know, "have you done now?"

What *had* I done? I wasn't sure.

"I have," I said, "a very bad feeling about this."

"Come on." Rob sighed tiredly. "Let's go find out."

They didn't want to let us in at the gate, of course. Rob had no visitor's pass, and the security guard looked down his nose at my employee ID and went, "Only time counselors are allowed to leave the camp is Sunday afternoons."

I looked at him like he was crazy. "I know that," I said. "I snuck out. Now are you going to let me back in, or not?"

You could totally tell the guy, who couldn't have been more than nineteen or twenty, had tried for the local police force and hadn't made it. So he'd opted to become a security guard, thinking that would give him the authority and respect he'd always yearned for. He sucked on his two overlarge front teeth and, peering at Rob and me, went, " 'Fraid not. There's a bit of a problem up at the camp, you know, and—"

I put down the face shield of my helmet and said to Rob, "Let's go."

Rob said to the security guard, "Nice talkin' to ya."

Then he gunned the engine, and we went around the red-and-white barrier arm, churning up quite a bit of dust and gravel as we did so. What did it matter? I couldn't get more fired than I already was.

The security guard came out of his little house and started yelling, but there wasn't much he could do to make us turn around. It wasn't like he had a gun, or anything.

Not that guns had ever stopped us before, of course.

As we drove up the long gravel road to the camp, I noticed how still and cool the woods were, especially with the coming rainstorm. The sky above us was clouding up more with every passing moment. You could smell the rain in the air, fresh and sweet.

Of course it wasn't until I was about to be kicked out of there that I'd finally begun to appreciate Camp Wawasee. It was too bad, really. I'd never even gotten a chance to float around the lake on an inner tube.

When we pulled up to the administrative offices, I was surprised at how many people were milling around. The squad cars were parked kind of haphazardly, and there was no sign of the cops who'd been driving them. They must, I figured, be inside, talking to Dr. Alistair, Pamela, and Ms. John Wayne.

But there were campers and counselors aplenty, which I thought was a little weird. If there'd been some sort of accident or crisis, you'd have thought they'd have tried to keep it from the kids. . . .

. . . And that's when I realized that they couldn't have kept it from the kids, even if they'd wanted to. It was five-thirty, and the kids and their counselors were streaming into the dining hall for supper. The dining staff prepared meals at exactly the same time every day, crisis or no crisis.

All of the kids were staring curiously at the squad cars. When they noticed Rob and me, they looked even more curious, and began whispering to one another. Oddly enough, I saw no members of Birch Tree Cottage in the crowds. . . .

But I saw a lot of other people I knew, including Ruth and Scott, who made no move whatsoever to approach me.

That's when I realized I still had my helmet on. Of course no one was saying hi. No one recognized me. As soon as I'd dragged the heavy thing off, Ruth came right over, and, as Rob pulled his helmet off as well, said, very sarcastically, "Well, I see you managed to find that ride you were looking for."

I shot her a warning look. Ruth can really be very snotty when she puts her mind to it.

"Ruth," I said. "I don't think I've ever formally introduced you to my friend, Rob. Ruth Abramowitz, this is Rob Wilkins. Rob, Ruth."

Rob nodded curtly to Ruth. "How you doing," he said.

Ruth smiled at him. It was not her best effort, by any means.

"I'm doing very well, thank you," she said primly. "And you?"

Rob, his eyebrows raised, said, "I'm good."

"Ruth." One of the residents of Tulip Tree Cottage pulled on Ruth's T-shirt. "I'm *hungry*. Can we go in now?"

Ruth turned and said to her campers, "You all go in now, and save a place for me. I'll be there in a minute."

The kids went away, with many glances not only at me and Rob, but at the squad cars. "What are the *police* doing here?" more than one of them asked loudly of no one in particular.

"Good question," I said to Ruth. "What *are* the police doing here?"

"I don't know." Ruth was still looking at Rob. She had seen him before, of course, back when he and I had had detention together. Ruth used to come pick me up, so my parents wouldn't find out about my somewhat checkered disciplinary record.

But I guess this was the first time she'd ever seen Rob from close up, and I could tell she was memorizing the details for later analysis. Ruth's like that.

"What do you mean, you don't know?" I

demanded. "The place is crawling with cops, and you don't know why?"

Ruth finally wrenched her gaze from Rob and fastened it onto me instead.

"No," she said. "I don't know. All I know is, we were down at the lake, having free swim and all, and the lifeguard blew his whistle and made us all go back inside."

"We thought it was on account of the storm," Scott said, nodding toward the still-darkening sky above us.

It was at this point that Karen Sue Hanky strolled up to us. I could tell by the expression on her pointy rat face that she had something important to tell us . . . and by the unnatural glitter in her baby-blue eyes, I knew it was something I wasn't going to like.

"Oh," she said, pretending she had only just noticed me. "I see you've decided to join us again." She glanced flirtatiously at Rob. "And brought along a friend, I see."

Even though Karen Sue had gone to school with Rob, she didn't recognize him. Girls like Karen Sue simply don't notice guys like Rob. I suppose she thought he was just some random local I'd picked up off the highway and brought back to camp for some recreational groping.

"Karen Sue," I said, "you better hurry and get into the dining hall. I heard a rumor they were running low on wheatgrass juice."

She just smiled at me, which wasn't a very good sign.

"Aren't you funny," Karen Sue said. "But then I suppose it's very amusing to you, what's going on. On account of it all being because of you telling that one little boy to hit that other little boy." Karen Sue flicked some of her hair back over her shoulder and sighed. "Well, I guess it just goes to show, violence doesn't pay."

Overhead, the clouds had gotten so thick, the sun was blocked out almost entirely. Inside the dining hall, the lights had come on, though this usually didn't happen until seven or eight o'clock, when the cleaning crew was at work. In the distance, thunder rumbled. The smell of ozone was heavy in the air.

I stepped forward until Karen Sue's upturned nose was just an inch from mine, and she stumbled back a step, tripping over a root and nearly falling flat on her face.

When she straightened, I asked her just what the heck she was talking about.

Only I didn't say heck.

Karen Sue started talking very quickly, and in a voice that was higher in pitch than usual.

"Well, I just went into the administrative offices for a second because I had to make sure the fax from Amber's doctor had come—about how her chronic ear infections prevent her from taking part in the Polar Bear swim—and I just happened to overhear the police talking to Dr. Alistair about how one of the boys from Birch Tree Cottage went to the lake, but no one saw him come out of it—"

I reached out and grabbed a handful of Karen

Sue's shirt, on account of how she was slowly backing farther and farther away from me.

"Who?" I demanded. Even though it was still about seventy-five degrees, in spite of the coming rainstorm, my skin was prickly with goose bumps. "Who went into the lake and didn't come out of it?"

"That one you were always yelling at," Karen Sue said. "Shane. Jessica, while you were gone"—she shook her head—"Shane *drowned.*"

CHAPTER

13

Thunder rumbled again, much closer this time. Now the hair on my arms was standing up not because I was cold, but because of all the electricity in the air.

I grabbed hold of Karen Sue's shirt with my other hand as well, and dragged her toward me. "What do you mean, *drowned?*"

"Just what I said." Karen Sue's voice was higher than ever. "Jess, he went into the lake and he never came out—"

"Bull," I said. "That's bull, Karen. Shane's a good swimmer."

"Well, when they blew the whistle for everyone to get out," Karen Sue said, her tone starting to sound a little hysterical, "Shane never came onto shore."

"Then he never went into the water in the first place," I hissed from between gritted teeth.

"Maybe," Karen Sue said. "And maybe if you'd been here, doing your job, and hadn't gone off with your boyfriend"—she sneered in Rob's direction—"you'd know."

Everything, the trees, the cloudy sky, the path, everything, seemed to be spinning around. It was like that scene in the *Wizard of Oz* when Dorothy wakes up in the tornado. Except that I was the only thing standing still.

"I don't believe you," I said again. I shook Karen Sue hard enough to make her pink headband snap off and go flying through the air. "You're lying. I ought to smash your face in, you—"

"All right." Suddenly, the world stopped spinning, and Rob was there, prying my fingers off Karen Sue's shirt. "All right, Mastriani, that's enough."

"You're lying," I said to Karen Sue. "You're a liar, and everyone knows it."

Karen Sue, white-faced and shaking, bent down, picked up her headband, and pushed it shakily back into place. There were some dead leaves stuck to it, but she apparently didn't notice.

I really wanted to jump her, knock her to the ground, and grind her rat face into the dirt. Only I couldn't get at her, because Rob had me around the waist, and wouldn't let go, no matter how hard I struggled to get away. If Mr. Goodhart had been there, he'd have been way disappointed in me. I seemed to have forgotten all the anger-management skills he'd taught me.

"You know what else, Karen Sue?" I shouted.

"You can't play flute for squat! They weren't even going to let you in here, with your lousy five out of ten on your performance score, except that Andrew Shippinger came down with mono, and they were *desperate*—"

"Okay," Rob said, lifting me up off my feet. "That's enough of that."

"That was supposed to be *my* cabin," I yelled at her, from over Rob's shoulder. "The Frangipanis were supposed to be *mine!*"

Rob had turned me around so that I was facing Ruth. She took one look at me and went, "Jess. Cool it."

I said fiercely, "He's *not* dead. He's *not.*"

Ruth blinked, then looked from me to Scott and back again. I looked at them, too, and realized from the way they were staring at me that something weird was going on with my face. I reached up to touch it, and felt wetness.

Great. I was crying. I was crying, and I hadn't even noticed.

"She's lying," I said one last time, but not very loudly.

Rob must have decided the fight had gone out of me, since he put me down—though he kept one hand glued to the back of my neck—and said, "There's one way to find out, isn't there?"

He nodded toward the administrative offices. I wiped my cheeks with the backs of my hands and said, "Okay."

Ruth insisted on following Rob and me, and Scott,

to my surprise, insisted on coming with her. It sunk into my numbed consciousness that there was something going on there, but I was too worried about Shane to figure it out just then. I'd think about it later. When we stepped into the building, the John Wayne look-alike secretary stood up and said, "Kids, they still don't know anything yet. I know you're worried, but if you could just stay with your campers—"

"Shane *is* my camper," I said.

The woman's thick eyebrows went up. She stared at me, apparently uncertain as to how best to reply.

I helped her out.

"Where are they?" I demanded, striding past her and down the hall. "Dr. Alistair's office?"

The secretary, scrambling out from behind her desk, went, "Oh, wait. You can't go back there—"

But it was too late. I'd already turned the corner and reached the door marked "Camp Director." I threw it open. Behind a wide desk sat the white-haired, red-faced Dr. Alistair. In various chairs and couches around his office sat Pamela, two state troopers, a sheriff's deputy, and the sheriff of Wawasee County himself.

"Jess." Pamela jumped to her feet. "There you are. Oh, thank God. We couldn't find you anywhere. And Dr. Alistair said you didn't show up for a meeting with him this afternoon—"

I looked at Pamela. What was she playing at? She, of all people, should have known where I was. Hadn't Jonathan Herzberg called and told her all about my returning his daughter to him?

I didn't think this was an appropriate time to bring that up, however. I said, "I was unavoidably detained. Can someone please tell me what's going on?"

Dr. Alistair stood up. He didn't look like a world-famous conductor anymore, or even a camp director. Instead, he looked like a frail old man, though he couldn't have been more than sixty years old.

"What's going on?" he echoed. "What's going on? You mean to say you don't know? Aren't you the famous psychic? How could you not know, with your special, magic powers? Hmm, Miss Mastriani?"

I glanced from Dr. Alistair to Pamela and back again. Had she told him? I supposed she must have.

But the astonished look on her face implied that she had not.

"I'll tell you what's going on, young lady," Dr. Alistair said, "since your psychic powers seem to be failing you at the moment. One of our campers is missing. Not just any camper, but one of the boys assigned to *your* care. Ostensibly, he's drowned. For the first time in our fifty-year history, we've had a death here at the camp."

I flinched as if he'd hit me. Not because of what he'd said, though that was bad enough. No, it was what he hadn't said, the thing that was implied in his tone:

That it was all my fault.

"But I'm surprised you didn't know that already." Dr. Alistair's tone was mocking. "Lightning Girl."

"Now, Hal," the sheriff said in a gruff voice. "Why

don't we just calm down here? We don't know that for sure. We don't have a body yet."

"The last time anyone saw him alive, he was on the way to the lake with the rest of his cabin. He isn't anywhere on the campgrounds. The boy's dead, I tell you. And it's entirely our fault! If his *counselor* had been there to keep an eye on him, it wouldn't have happened."

My throat was dry. I tried to swallow, but couldn't. Outside, lightning flashed, followed almost immediately by a long roll of thunder.

Then the heavens unloosed. Rain beat against the windows behind Dr. Alistair's desk. One of the state troopers, looking out at the downpour, said, in a morose voice, "Gonna be hard to drag that lake now."

Drag the lake? *Drag the lake?*

"Wasn't there a lifeguard?"

Rob. Rob was trying to help. Rob was trying to deflect some of the blame from me. Sweet of him, of course, but a useless effort. It was my fault. If I'd been there, Shane never would have drowned. I wouldn't have let him.

"It seems to me," Rob said reasonably, "if the kid was swimming, there ought to have been a lifeguard. Wouldn't the lifeguard have noticed someone drowning on his watch?"

Dr. Alistair squinted at him through the lenses of his bifocals. "Who," he demanded, "are you?" Then he spied Ruth and Scott in the doorway. "What is this?" he demanded. "Who are you people? This is my private office. Get out."

None of them moved, although Ruth looked like she really wanted to run somewhere far away. Somewhere where there weren't any sheriff deputies or angry camp directors. It was just like the time her brother Skip had been stung by the bee, only instead of someone going into anaphylactic shock, someone—namely me—was dying a slower death . . . of guilt.

"Well," Rob said. "Wasn't there a lifeguard?"

The sheriff said, "There was. He didn't notice anything unusual."

"That's because," I said, more to myself than anyone else, "Shane never went into the water." It wasn't something I knew with any certainty. Just something I suspected.

But that didn't stop Dr. Alistair from looking at me from behind his wire-rimmed glasses and demanding, "And I suppose, since you weren't there, you're able to tell that using your special powers?"

It was at this point that Rob took a step toward Dr. Alistair's desk. The sheriff put out a hand, however, and said, "Easy, son." Then, to Dr. Alistair, he said, "Just what are you talking about, Hal?"

"Oh, you don't recognize her?" Dr. Alistair looked prim. I wondered if maybe losing a camper had sent him around the bend. He'd never been one of the most stable people, anyway, if his erratic behavior during all-camp rehearsal had been any indication: Dr. Alistair frequently became so enraged with the horn section, he threw his conducting baton at them, only missing because they'd learned to duck.

"Jessica Mastriani," he went on, "the girl with the psychic power to find missing people. Of course it's a little late for her help now, isn't it? Considering the fact that the boy's already dead."

"Oh, Hal." Pamela stood up. "We don't know that. He might just have run away." She looked at me. "Wasn't there some altercation earlier today?"

I nodded, remembering the tick incident, and the fact that I had refused to give Lionel a strike for punching Shane.

More than that, however, I remembered the look Shane had given me when I'd lied to him about that photo of Taylor Monroe. He hadn't believed me. He hadn't believed a word I'd said.

Was this his way of getting back at me for lying to him?

If only, I thought, I could go to sleep right now. If I went to sleep right now, I'd be able to find out exactly where Shane was. Maybe if I could get Dr. Alistair really mad, he'd clock me with his baton, the way he was always trying to clock the horn players. Could I find missing kids while unconscious? Was that the same as being asleep?

Probably not. And I doubted the sheriff would let Dr. Alistair clock me, anyway. Rob definitely wouldn't. I wondered if protectiveness was listed as one of the "10 Ways to Tell He Thinks of You as More Than Just a Friend."

Like it mattered now. Now that it looked as if I might have killed a kid. Well, indirectly, anyway.

"What about the other boys from Birch Tree

Cottage?" I asked. "Did anybody talk to them? Ask them if they'd seen Shane?" Dave? Where was Dave? He'd promised to look after them. . . .

"We've got some officers interviewing them now," the sheriff said to me. "In their cabin. But so far . . . nothing."

"He was last seen on his way to the lake with the others," Dr. Alistair insisted stubbornly.

"Doesn't mean he drowned," Rob pointed out.

Dr. Alistair looked at him. "Who," he wanted to know, "are you? You're not one of the counselors." He looked at Pamela. "He's not one of the counselors, is he, Pamela?"

Pamela reached up to run a hand through her short blond hair. "No, Hal," she said tiredly. "He's not."

"He's my friend," I said. I didn't say Rob was my boyfriend because, well, he's not. Plus I thought it might look even worse than it already did, me being gone for hours, then showing up with some random guy in tow. "And we were just leaving."

But my efforts to cover up the truth about my feelings for Rob proved to be for nothing as Dr. Alistair said, pretty nastily, "Leaving? Oh, well, isn't that special. You seem to have a knack, Miss Mastriani, for being unavailable when you're needed most."

My mouth fell open. What *was* this? I wondered. If he was going to fire me, why didn't he just get it over with? I had to hurry up and get to sleep if we were ever going to find Shane.

"What about those special powers of yours?" Dr.

Alistair went on. "Don't you feel the slightest obligation to help us find this boy?"

Even then, I still didn't get what was going on. I just thought Dr. Alistair was crazy, or something.

I think Rob must have felt the same thing, because he reached out and grabbed one of my arms, just above the elbow, like he was going to pull me out of the way if Dr. Alistair whipped out that baton and started firing.

I went, "I don't have special powers anymore, Dr. Alistair."

"Oh?" Dr. Alistair's shaggy white eyebrows went up. "Is that so? *Then where were you all afternoon?*"

I felt my stomach drop, as if I'd been on an elevator. Except, of course, that I wasn't. How had he known? *How had he known?*

"Okay," Rob said, steering me toward the door—I guess because I was so stunned, I wasn't moving. "We're going now."

"You can't go anywhere!" Dr. Alistair thumped on his desk with his fist. "You are an employee of Lake Wawasee Camp for Gifted Child Musicians, and you—"

Something finally got through the haze of confusion his question about where I'd been all afternoon had cast around me. And that something was the fact that he was still speaking to me as if I worked for him.

"Not anymore," I interrupted. "I mean, I'm fired, aren't I?"

Dr. Alistair looked alarmed. "Fired?" at the same

time as Pamela said, "Oh, Jess, of course not. None of this is your fault."

Not fired? *Not fired?* How could I be not fired? I had taken off for hours, without offering a single explanation as to where I'd been. And while I'd been gone, one of the kids in my charge had disappeared. And I *wasn't fired?*

The uncomfortable feeling that had been creeping over me since I'd set foot in Dr. Alistair's office got stronger than ever. And suddenly I knew what I had to do.

"If I'm not fired," I said, "then I quit. Come on, Rob."

Pamela looked stricken. "Oh, Jess. You can't—"

"You can't quit," Dr. Alistair cried. "You signed a contract!"

He said a bunch of other things, but I didn't wait to hear them. I left. I just walked out.

Rob and the others followed me out into the waiting area. The John-Waynish secretary was there, talking on the phone. She lowered her voice when she saw us, but didn't hang up.

"Are you crazy, Jess?" Ruth wanted to know. "Quitting, when you didn't have to? They weren't going to fire you, you know."

"I know," I said. "That's why I had to quit. Who would want to hang on to an employee like me? I'll tell you who: someone with ulterior motives."

"I don't really understand any of this." Scott, speaking for the first time, looked concerned. "And it probably isn't any of my business. But it seems to me if you really do have psychic powers and all of that, and people want you to use them, shouldn't you, I don't know, do it? I mean, you could probably make a lot of money at it."

Rob and I just stared at him incredulously. Ruth's look was more pitying.

"Oh," she said. "You poor thing."

It was right then that the double glass doors to the administrative building blew open. We all backed out of the way as two people, holding dripping umbrellas, stepped into the office waiting room.

It wasn't until they shook the umbrellas closed that I recognized them. And when I did, I groaned.

"Oh, jeez," I said. "Not you again."

CHAPTER

14

"**J**ess." Special Agent Smith shook rainwater from her hair. "We need to talk."

I couldn't believe it. I really couldn't. I mean, it is one thing to have the FBI following you wherever you go.

But it is quite another to have the people who are supposed to be anonymous tails come up and start talking to you. It simply isn't done. Everyone knows *that*. I mean, how uncool can you get?

"Look," I said, holding up my right hand. "I really don't have time for this right now. I am having a personal crisis, and—"

"It's going to become really personal," Special Agent Johnson said—his lips, I noticed, looked thinner than usual—"if Clay Larsson gets his hands on you."

"Clay Larsson?" I tried to think who they were

talking about. Then it dawned on me. "You mean Keely's new dad?"

"Right." Special Agent Johnson threw Rob a look. "His cousin's mother's boyfriend."

Rob screwed up his face and went, "My what?"

I didn't blame him. I was confused, too.

"After you left him this afternoon," Special Agent Johnson explained, "Mr. Larsson rightly guessed that the person who had kidnapped his girlfriend's daughter was someone who'd been hired by the child's father. He therefore paid a little visit to your friend Mr. Herzberg, who returned to his office after his rendezvous with you at the McDonald's."

"Oh." God, I'm a moron sometimes. "Is he . . . I mean, he's all right and everything, right?"

"He's got a broken jaw." Special Agent Johnson referred to the notepad he always carries around. "Three fractured ribs, a concussion, a dislocated knee, and a severely contused hip bone."

"Oh, my God." I was shocked. "Keely—"

"Keely is fine." Special Agent Smith's voice was soothing. "We have her in protective custody, where she'll remain while Mr. Larsson is still at large."

I raised my eyebrows. "You guys didn't catch him?"

"We might have," Special Agent Johnson pointed out—rather nastily, if you ask me, "if certain people had been a bit more forthcoming about their activities earlier today."

"Whoa," I said. "You are *not* pinning this on me. It

doesn't have anything to do with me. I'm just an innocent bystander in this one—"

"Jess." Special Agent Johnson frowned down at me. "We know. Jonathan Herzberg told us everything."

My mouth fell open. I couldn't believe it. That rat! That dirty rat!

It was Rob who asked suspiciously, "He told you everything, did he? With a broken jaw?"

Special Agent Johnson flipped back a few pages in his notepad, then showed it to us. There, in shaky handwriting I didn't recognize—it certainly wasn't Allan Johnson's precise script—was Jonathan Herzberg's version of the events leading up to his assault by his ex-wife's boyfriend. My name appeared frequently.

The louse. The louse had ratted me out. I couldn't believe it. After everything I'd done for him . . .

"Jess." Special Agent Smith, in her powder blue suit, looked more like a real estate broker than she did an FBI agent. I guess that was the point. "Clay Larsson is not a particularly stable individual. He has an arrest record a mile long. Assault and battery, resisting arrest, assaulting a police officer . . . He is a very dangerous and volatile person, and from what Mr. Herzberg tells us, we have reason to believe that, at this point in time, he has a particular grudge against . . . well, against you, Jess."

Considering the foot I'd smashed into his face, I could readily believe this. Still, it wasn't as if Clay Larsson knew who I was, much less where I lived.

"Well, that's just the thing," Special Agent Smith said, when I voiced these thoughts. "He *does* know, Jess. You see, he . . . well, he pretty much tortured Keely's father until he told him."

Rob said, "Okay. That's it. Let's go get your stuff, Mastriani. We're out of here."

It took me longer than it had taken Rob to digest what I'd just heard, though. Clay Larsson, who clearly had even worse anger-management issues than I did, knew who I was and where I lived, and was coming after me to exact revenge for (a) kicking him in the face, and (b) kidnapping his girlfriend's daughter, whom she, in turn, had kidnapped from her ex-husband?

How did I ever get to be so lucky? Really. I want to know. I mean, have you ever, in your life, met anyone with worse luck than mine?

"Well," I said. "That's great. That's just great. And I suppose you two are here to protect me?"

Special Agent Johnson put his notepad away, and when he did, I saw that his pistol was in its shoulder holster, ready for action.

"That's one way of putting it," he said. "It is in the national interest to keep you alive, Jess, despite your assertions that you no longer possess the, er, talent that originally brought you to the attention of our superiors. We're just going to hang around here and make sure that, if Mr. Larsson makes it onto Camp Wawasee property, you are protected."

"The best way to protect Jess," Rob said, "would be to get her out of here."

"Precisely," Agent Johnson said. He looked Rob up and down, like he was seeing him for the first time—which I guess he was, up close, anyway. The two of them were about the same size—a fact which seemed to surprise Agent Johnson a little. For somebody who was supposed to be inconspicuous, the agent was pretty tall.

"We're planning on taking her to a safe house until Mr. Larsson has been captured," he said to Rob.

"I don't think so," Rob said at the same time that Ruth, standing behind him, went, "Oh, no. Not again."

"Excuse me," I said to Special Agent Johnson. "But don't you remember the last time you guys took me somewhere I was supposed to be safe?"

Special Agents Johnson and Smith exchanged glances. Agent Smith said, "Jess, this time, I promise you—"

"No way," I said. "I'm not going anywhere with you two. Besides"—I looked out the double glass doors at the rain which was still streaming down— "I've got some unfinished business here."

"Jess," Special Agent Smith began.

"No, Jill," I said. Don't ask me when my relationship with Special Agents Johnson and Smith had graduated to a first-name basis. I think it was around the time I'd bought them their first double cheeseburger meal. "I'm not going anywhere. I have things to do here. Responsibilities."

"Jessica," Special Agent Smith said. "This really isn't the time to—"

"I mean it," I said. "I have to go."

And I went. I walked right out of there, right out into the rain. It was still coming down—not as hard as before, maybe, but there was plenty of it. It only took a few seconds for my shirt and jeans to get soaked.

I didn't care. I hadn't lied to them. I had things to do. Finding Shane, wherever he was, was first and foremost on my list. Was he out, I wondered, as I stalked with my head bent in the direction of Birch Tree Cottage, in this storm? Had he found shelter somewhere? Was he dry? Was he warm? Did I even care? As many times as I'd wanted to wring his stupid neck—and I'd thought about it, fairly seriously, several times a day—did I really care what happened to him?

Yeah, I did. And not just because that oversized Mullet Head was capable of making such beautiful music. But because, well, I sort of liked him. Surprising, but true. I liked the annoying little freak.

Thunder rumbled overhead, though it was farther away than before. Then Rob came jogging up behind me.

"That was some dramatic exit," he said. His shirt and jeans, I noted, were also quickly becoming soaked.

"My specialty," I said.

"You're going the wrong way."

I stopped in the middle of the path and looked around, forgetting for a second that Rob had never been to Camp Wawasee, and so would have no way of knowing which way was the right way to Birch Tree Cottage.

"No, I'm not," I said.

"Yes, you are." He jerked a thumb over his shoulder. "The bike's that way."

I realized what he meant, then shook my head. "Rob," I said. "I can't leave."

"Jess."

Rob hardly ever calls me by my first name. More often than not, he refers to me the way he used to in detention, where we were, basically, nothing but discipline files, badly in need of sorting—by last name only.

So when he does call me by my first name, it usually means he's being very serious about something. In this case, it appeared to be my personal safety.

Unfortunately, I had no choice but to disappoint him.

"No," I said. "No, Rob. I'm not going."

He didn't say anything right away. I squinted up at him, the rain making it hard to see. He was looking down at me, his pale blue eyes filled with something I couldn't quite put my finger on. Not love, certainly.

"Jess," he said in a low, even voice. "You know I think you're a pretty down girl. You know that, don't you?"

I blinked. It wasn't easy to look up at him, with all that rain coming down in my eyes. Plus it was pretty dark. The only way I could see him was in the light from one of the lamps along the pathways, and that was pretty dim.

But he certainly looked serious.

I nodded. "Okay," I said. "We'll call that one a given, if you want."

"Good," he said. The rain had plastered his dark hair to his face and scalp, but he didn't seem to notice. "Then maybe when I say this next part, you'll understand where I'm coming from. I did not drive all the way up here to watch you get your brains hacked out by some psycho, okay? Now you get that ass"—he pointed to the one in question—"on my bike, or I swear to God, I'm going to put it there for you."

Now I knew what was in his eyes. And it wasn't love. Oh, definitely not.

It was anger.

I wiped rainwater from my eyes.

And then I said the only thing I could say: "No."

He made that half-disgusted, half-amused smile he seems to wear fifty percent of the time he's with me, then looked off into the distance for a second . . . though what he saw out there, I couldn't say. All I could see was rain.

"I have to find Shane," I shouted above a rumble of thunder.

"Yeah?" He looked down at me, still smiling. "I don't give a crap about Shane."

Anger bubbled, hot and dark, inside me. I tried to tamp it down. Count to ten, I told myself. Mr. Goodhart had suggested a long time ago that I count to ten when I felt like slugging someone. Sometimes it even worked.

"Well, I do," I said. "And I'm not leaving here until I know he's safe."

He stopped smiling.

I should have guessed what was coming next. Rob's not the kind of guy who goes around saying stuff just to hear himself talk.

Still, he's never gotten physical with me before. Not the way he did then.

I like to think that, if it had come down to it, I could have gotten away. I really think I could have. Okay, yeah, he had me upside down, which is pretty disorienting. Also, my arms were pinned, which certainly puts a girl at a disadvantage.

But I am thoroughly convinced that, with a few well-placed head-butts—if I could have gotten my head near his, which I am convinced I could have, given enough time—I could have gotten away.

Unfortunately, our tender interlude in the woods was interrupted before I was able to bring it to any sort of head-butting climax.

"Son." Special Agent Johnson's voice rang out through the rain and mist. "Put the girl down."

Rob was already striding purposefully toward his bike. He did not even slow down.

"I don't think so," was all he said.

Then Special Agent Johnson stepped out from between the trees. Even though I was upside down, I could still see he had his gun drawn—which surprised me, I must say.

It seemed to surprise Rob, too, since he froze, and stood there for a second or two. Now that I was upside down, I began to realize that my previous assumption—you know, that I was soaked—had actually been erroneous. I was not soaked. There had been no rainwater, for instance, on my stomach.

But now that I was upside down, there certainly was.

And might I add that this was not a pleasant sensation?

"You," Rob said to Special Agent Johnson, "are not going to shoot me. What if you hit her?"

"It would be unfortunate," Special Agent Johnson said, "but since she has been a thorn in my side since the day we met, it wouldn't upset me too much."

"Allan!" I was shocked. "What would Mrs. Johnson say if she could hear you now?"

"Put her down, son."

Rob flipped me over, and put me back on my feet. While this was happening, Special Agent Johnson came up and took my arm. He still had his gun out, to my surprise. But he was pointing it into the air.

"Now get on your motorcycle, Mr. Wilkins," he said to Rob, "and go home."

"Hey." Now that some of the blood was receding from my head, I could think straight. "How did you know his last name? I never told you that."

Special Agent Johnson looked bored. "License plate."

"Oh," I said.

I glanced back at Rob, standing in the rain, with

his T-shirt all sticking to him. You could see his abs through the drenched material. It occurred to me that this, too, was like a scene from a music video. You know, the totally hot guy standing in the rain after his girlfriend dumps him?

Except that I so totally was not dumping him. I was just trying to find a kid. That was all.

Only nobody was letting me.

Then something else occurred to me: If Rob's T-shirt was that wet, then what about mine?

I looked down, and promptly folded my arms across my chest.

It was better this way, I thought. I mean, not about our wet T-shirts, but the fact that they were making him go away. Because I knew it would be a lot easier to ditch the Wonder Twins than it would Rob. FBI agents I didn't mind head-butting. But when it came down to it, I think hurting Rob would have been hard.

"I'll call you," I said to Rob over my shoulder, as Special Agent Johnson started to pull me back toward the center of the camp.

"Do me a favor, Mastriani," Rob said.

"Sure," I said. It was hard to walk backward through the rain, but Special Agent Johnson was pulling so hard on me, I didn't have much choice. "What?"

"Don't."

And then Rob turned and started walking away. It didn't take long for the rain and mist to swallow him up. A minute later, I heard the engine of his Indian rev up.

And then he was gone.

I looked up at Special Agent Johnson, who, unlike Rob, did not look sexy drenched in rainwater.

"I hope you're happy now," I said to him. "That guy might have been my boyfriend someday, if you hadn't come along and ruined it."

Special Agent Johnson was busy dialing some numbers on his cell phone. He said, "Do your parents know about you and Mr. Wilkins, Jess?"

"Of course they do," I said very indignantly. "Though I have my own life, you know. My parents do not dictate whom I see or do not see socially."

This was such an outrageous string of lies, I'm surprised my tongue didn't shrivel up and fall off.

Special Agent Johnson didn't look like he believed any of them, either.

"Do your parents know," he went on, as if our conversation hadn't been interrupted, "that Mr. Wilkins has an arrest record? And is currently on probation?"

"Yes," I said, as sassily as I could. Then, because I couldn't resist, I went, "Although they aren't too clear on just what he's on probation for. . . ."

Special Agent Johnson just looked down at me, frowning a little. He went, "That information is, of course, confidential. If Mr. Wilkins has not chosen to share it with . . . your parents, I don't see that I can."

Jeez! Shot down again! How was I *ever* going to find out what Rob had done to land him in the cinderblock jungle? Rob wouldn't tell me, and, not surprisingly, I couldn't get a straight answer out of the

Feds, either. It couldn't have been that bad, or he'd have served time and not just gotten probation. But what *was* it?

It didn't look like I'd ever find out now. No, I'd managed to ruin that little relationship, hadn't I?

But what was I supposed to do? I mean, really?

Whoever was on the other end of Special Agent Johnson's cell phone must have picked up, since he said into it, "Cassie secured. Repeat, Cassie secured."

Then he hung up.

"Who," I demanded, "is Cassie?"

"I beg your pardon," Special Agent Johnson said, putting his phone away. "I ought to have said Cassandra."

"And who's Cassandra?"

"No one you need to worry about."

I glared at him. Now that I'd been out in the rain so long, I didn't even care how wet I was. I mean, it wasn't like I couldn't get any wetter.

Or more miserable.

"Wait a minute," I said. "I remember now. Seventh grade. We did mythology. Cassandra was like a psychic, or something."

"She had a talent," Special Agent Johnson admitted, "for prophecy."

"Yeah," I said. "Only she was under this curse, and—" I shook my head in disbelief. "*That's* my code name? *Cassandra?*"

"You'd have preferred something else?"

"Yeah," I said. "How about no code name?"

I was having, I decided, a pretty bad day. First a

psycho wife-beater tries to kill me, then my boy-friend walks out on me. Now I find out I have a code name with the FBI. What next?

Special Agent Smith appeared from the shadows, sheltered under a big black umbrella.

"Look at you two," she said when she saw us. "You're soaked." She moved until the umbrella was covering all three of us. Well, more or less.

"I managed to secure some rooms," she said, "at a Holiday Inn a few miles away. I don't think Mr. Larsson will think to look for Jess there."

"Do I get my own room?" I asked hopefully.

"Of course not." Special Agent Smith smiled at me. "We're roomies."

Great. "I'm a remote hog," I informed her.

"I'll live," she said.

This was horrible. This was terrible. I couldn't go stay in a cushy Holiday Inn while Shane was out in the wilderness somewhere . . . or worse, dead. I had to find him.

Only how was I going to do that? How was I going to find him, and not let Allan and Jill know what I was up to?

"I have to," I said, my throat dry, "get my stuff."

"Of course." Special Agent Johnson looked at his watch. It was one of those ones that light up. "We'll escort you back to your cabin to gather your belong-ings."

Jeez!

Still, I think Special Agents Johnson and Smith began to regret their assignment to Project Cassandra more than ever when we stepped into Birch Tree Cottage and observed the level of chaos there. The kids were off the wall. When we walked in, we narrowly escaped being hit by a flying chunk of bow rosin. Arthur was playing his tuba, in spite of the no-practicing-outside-of-the-music-building rule; Lionel was screaming for silence at the top of his lungs; Doo Sun and Tony were sword-fighting with a pair of violin bows . . .

And in the middle of it all, a lady police officer was standing with her hands over her ears, pleading ineffectively with her charges: "Please! Please listen to me, we're going to find your friend—"

I strode into the kitchen, opened the fuse box, and threw the switches.

Plunged into semi-darkness, the boys froze. All noise ceased.

Then I stepped out from the kitchen—

—and instantly became part of a Jessica sandwich as all of the boys surrounded me, clinging to various parts of my body and crying my name.

"All right," I yelled, after a while. "Simmer down. Simmer down!"

I disentangled myself from their embrace, then sank down onto a bed—Shane's empty bed, I saw, when lightning again lit the now darkened room. The bed was haphazardly made, with musical note sheets. Shane would have preferred, I was fairly certain, bedding emblazoned with football paraphernalia. Nevertheless, the sheets gave off a Shane-like odor that, for once, I found comforting.

"All right," I said, interrupting the cries of "Jess, where have you been?" and "Didja hear about Shane?"

"Yes, I heard about Shane," I said. "Now I want to hear your version of what happened."

The boys looked at one another blankly, then shrugged, more or less in unity.

"He was with us on the way to the lake," Sam volunteered.

Lionel's accent worsened, I realized, when he was stressed. It took me a minute to figure out his next words: "But I think he did not go in the water."

"Really, Lionel?" I peered down at the little boy. "Why do you think that?"

"If Shane had gone into the water," Lionel said thoughtfully, "he would have tried to push my head under. But he did not."

"So he didn't actually make it into the lake?" I asked.

The boys shrugged again. Only Lionel nodded with anything like assurance.

"I think," Lionel said, "that Shane ran away. He was very angry with you, Jess, for not giving me the strike."

As usual, he pronounced my name Jace. And, as usual, Lionel was right. At least I thought so. I think Shane had been angry with me . . . angry enough that maybe—just maybe—he wanted to teach me a lesson.

Shane, I thought to myself. Where are you? And what are you up to?

Suddenly, the lights came back on. Special Agent Smith came out of the kitchen, then nodded toward my room. "Are those your belongings in there?"

I nodded.

"I'll pack them for you," she said, and disappeared into my room, while her partner leaned against the front doorjamb and looked at his watch again.

"Who's that guy?" Tony wanted to know.

"Is that your *boyfriend?*" Doo Sun asked.

"Is that *Rob?*" Arthur started to ask, but I slapped a hand over his mouth . . . probably as much to my own surprise as his.

"Shhh," I said. "That's not Rob. That's just a, um, friend of mine."

"Oh," Arthur said, when I'd removed my hand. "Have you been eating McDonald's?"

I picked up Shane's pillow and lowered my face into it. Oh, Lord, I prayed. Give me the strength not to kill any more little boys today. One is really enough, I think.

Special Agent Smith came out of my room, holding a duffel bag.

"I think I've got everything," she said. "Are these Gogurts yours, or should I leave them for the children?"

Arthur, his eyes very bright, swiveled his head toward me.

"Hey," he said. "What is she doing? Is that your stuff?"

"Are you leaving?" Lionel's chin began to tremble. "Are *you* going, Jace?"

Exasperated—this was *not* how I'd wanted to break the news to the boys that I was leaving—I said to Special Agent Smith, "The Gogurts and the cookies and the chips and stuff aren't mine. Don't pack them."

Special Agent Smith looked confused. "There are no cookies, Jess. Just these Gogurt things."

"No cookies?" I stared at her. "There should be. There should be cookies and chips and Fiddle Faddle."

"Fiddle *what?*" Special Agent Smith looked more confused than ever.

"Fiddle Faddle," the boys shouted at her.

"No." Special Agent Smith blinked. "None of that. Just these Gogurts."

Still clutching Shane's pillow, I stood up and looked down at the boys.

"Did you guys eat all that candy and stuff I confiscated from you the other day?"

They looked at one another. I could have sworn they had no idea what I was talking about.

"No," they said, shaking their heads.

"I tried," Arthur confessed. "But I couldn't reach it. You put it up too high."

Too high for Arthur.

But not, I realized, for the largest resident of Birch Tree Cottage . . . besides me, of course.

I became aware of several things all at once. One, that Ruth and Scott—followed by Dave—were stepping up onto the front porch . . . come to say good-bye, I guessed.

Two, the rain outside had suddenly stopped. There was only the most distant rumbling from the sky now, as the storm moved out toward Lake Michigan.

And three, the smell from Shane's pillow, which I still clutched, had become overwhelming.

And that was because all at once, I knew where he was.

And it wasn't at the bottom of Lake Wawasee.

CHAPTER

15

Look, what do you want me to say? I don't understand this psychic stuff any more than you do. Back when I'd been a special guest at Crane Military Base, they'd run a bunch of tests on me, and basically what they'd found out was that when I slip into REM-stage sleep, something happens to me. It's like the webmaster of my brain suddenly downloads some information that wasn't there before. That's how, when I wake up, I know stuff.

Only this time, it had happened while I was awake. Really. Right while I was standing there clutching Shane's stinky pillow.

And I hadn't felt a thing. In the comic books my brother Douglas is always reading, whenever one of the characters gets a psychic vision—and they do, frequently—he scrunches up his face and goes, "*Uhnnnn . . .*"

Seriously. *Uhnnn.* Like it hurts.

But I am telling you, downloading a psychic vision—or however they come—doesn't hurt. It's like one second the information is not there, and a second later, it is.

Like an e-mail.

Which was why, when I looked up from that pillow, it was really hard to contain myself. I mean, I didn't want to shout out what I knew for Special Agents Johnson and Smith to hear. I wasn't exactly anxious to let them in on this new development, considering all the time and effort I'd spent, assuring them I'd lost all psychic power entirely.

Still, when I finally did get a chance to impart what seemed, to me, like some pretty miraculous stuff, no one was very impressed.

"A *cave?*" Ruth's voice rose to a panic-stricken pitch. "You want me to go into a *cave* to look for that miserable kid? No, thanks."

I shushed her. I mean, it wasn't like the Feds weren't in the next room, or anything.

"Not you," I said. "I'll do the actual, um, cave entering." I didn't want to offend her by telling her the truth, which was that Ruth was the last person I'd ever pick to go spelunking with.

"But a *cave?*" Ruth still looked skeptical. "Why would he run off and hide in a cave?"

"Two words," I said. "Paul Huck."

"Who," Ruth whispered, "or should I say, *what* is a Paul Huck?"

"He's a guy who ran away to a cave," I explained quietly, "when he felt he was being persecuted."

We had to talk in whispers, because we were sequestered in my tiny cubicle of a bedroom, while outside, Special Agents Johnson and Smith sat guarding the perimeter. I was supposed to be saying good-bye to the boys and my friends. The Feds had very generously allotted me ten minutes to do this. I suppose their line of thinking was, Well, she can't get up to much trouble in that tiny room, now can she?

What they did not know, however, was that (a) the window in my tiny room actually opened wide enough for just about any size body to slip through, (b) two bodies had already slipped through it, in order to perform a small favor for me, and (c) instead of saying good-bye, like I was supposed to be doing, to Ruth and Scott and Dave, I was waiting for an opportunity to sneak out and find Shane, whom I knew now was not only not dead, but still on Camp Wawasee property.

"Remember," I whispered to Ruth, "at the first Pit, when they read off the rules and regulations? One of them was that Wolf Cave was off-limits. What kid, hearing about Paul Huck and feeling persecuted himself, isn't going to make a beeline for that cave? Plus he took all the junk food, *and* my flashlight is missing."

Ruth went, in this very meaningful tone, "Do you have any *other* reason to suspect he might be there, Jess?"

The surprising answer was, "Yes."

Ruth raised her eyebrows. "Really? What about all

that stuff about how you need to enter REM-stage sleep in order to achieve . . . you know?"

"I don't know," I said. "Maybe I don't need it, if I'm worked up enough. . . ."

I didn't know how to put into words what had happened when I'd hugged Shane's pillow. How the smell of his shampoo had filled my head with an image of him, huddled in the glow of a flashlight, and stuffing his face with Fiddle Faddle.

I don't know how it had happened, or if it would ever happen again. But I had had a vision, while wide-awake, of a missing person. . . .

And I was going to act on that vision, and right what I'd made wrong.

"If you ask me," Ruth said, "the stupid kid isn't worth the trouble."

"Ruth." I shook my head at her. "What kind of Camp Wawasee attitude is that?"

"He's a pill," Ruth said.

"You wouldn't say that," I assured her, "if you'd ever heard him play."

"He can't be that good."

"He is. Believe me." The memory of the hauntingly beautiful music Shane had played was as sharp in my head as the vision I'd had of him, shoveling Doritos into his mouth by flashlight.

Ruth sighed. "If you say so. Still, if I were you, I'd let him stay out there and rot. He'll come back on his own when the food runs out."

"Ruth, a kid got lost in that cave and died, remember? That's why it's off-limits. For all I know, Shane might not be able to find his way out, and that's why he's still in there."

Ruth looked skeptical. "And what makes you think you'll be able to find your way out, if he can't?"

I tapped my head. "My built-in guidance system."

"Oh, right," Ruth said. "I forgot. You and my dad's Mercedes."

Suddenly, the stillness that had fallen over the camp after the heavy rainstorm was ripped apart by an explosion so loud it made thunder sound like a finger-snap. Ruth clapped her hands over her ears.

"Whoa," I said, impressed. "Right on cue. That boyfriend of yours sure knows how to create a diversion."

Ruth lowered her hands and went primly, "Scott isn't my boyfriend." Then she added, "Yet. And he should know about diversions. He was an Eagle Scout, after all."

The door to my bedroom flew open. Special Agent Smith stood there, gun drawn.

"Thank God you're all right," she said when she saw me. Her blue eyes were wide with anxiety. "That can only be him. Clay Larsson, I mean. Stay here while Agent Johnson and I go to investigate, all right? We're leaving Officer Deckard and one of the sheriff's deputies, too—"

"Sure," I said calmly. "You go on."

Special Agent Smith gave me a nervous smile I suppose she meant to be reassuring. Then she shut the door.

I stood up. "Let's get out of here," I said, and headed for the window.

"I hope you know what you're doing," Ruth muttered unhappily as she followed me. "You know, they're probably overreacting with this whole Clay Larsson thing, but what if he really is, you know, out there, looking for you?"

I gave her a disgusted look over my shoulder before I dropped out the window. "Ruth," I said. "It's me you're talking to. You think I can't handle one little old wife-beater?"

"Well," Ruth said. "If you're going to put it *that* way . . ."

We slithered out the window as quietly as we could. Outside, except for a mysterious bright orange glow from the parking lot, it was dark. It wasn't as hot as it had been, thanks to the rain.

But everything, everything was wet. My sneakers, and the cuffs of my jeans, which had only just started to dry off, were soon soaked again. Drops of water fell down from the treetops every time a breeze stirred the leaves overhead. It was quite unpleasant . . . as Ruth did not hesitate to point out, at her first opportunity.

"My ankles itch," she whispered.

"No one said you had to come," I whispered back.

"Oh, sure," Ruth hissed. "Leave me behind to deal with the cops. Thanks a lot."

"If you're going to come with me, you have to quit complaining."

"Okay. Except that all of this rain is making my allergies act up."

I swear to you, sometimes I think it would be easier if I just didn't have a best friend.

We'd only gone about a dozen yards when we heard it—footsteps swiftly approaching us. I hissed at Ruth to put out her flashlight, but it turned out our caution had been for nothing, since it was only Scott and Dave, hurrying to join us.

"Hey," I said to them as they came trotting up. "Good job, you guys. They totally fell for it."

Scott ducked his head modestly. "You were right, Jess," he said. "Tampons do make good fuses."

I glanced at Ruth. "And you said detention was a waste of my time."

Ruth only shook her head. "The American public education system," she said, "was clearly not designed with ingrates like you in mind."

Dave glanced over his shoulder at the thick black smoke pouring from the parking lot into the night sky.

"Oh, I don't know," he said. He was panting, smudged with dirt, and covered in dead leaves and clearly exhilarated. I knew what he was thinking: Never, in his seventeen years of trumpet-playing, Dungeons-&-Dragon-dice-throwing geekdom, had he ever done anything so dangerous . . . and fun. "I was going to see if I could get extra credit for this from my chemistry teacher next semester. Lighting a van on fire with a Molotov cocktail has to be good for at least ten bonus points."

"You guys," Ruth said, "are insane."

Scott looked wounded. "Hey," he said. "We used

appropriate caution. No children or animals were harmed in the execution of this prank."

"No law enforcement officials, either," Dave added.

"I am surrounded," Ruth murmured, "by lunatics."

"Enough already," I whispered. "Let's go."

We ended up not actually needing our flashlights to see our way around the lake. The storm had passed, leaving behind a sky that was mostly clear. A shiny new moon shone down on us—just a sliver, but it shed enough of a glow for us to see by, at least while there were no trees overhead to block its light—along with a light dusting of stars.

If I hadn't realized it before, from the allergy remark, I knew by the time we were halfway around the lake that bringing Ruth along had been a big mistake. She simply would not shut up . . . and not because she wanted the whole world to know about her itching, watery eyes, but because she wanted Scott to know how big and brave she thought he was, taking on the FBI all by himself . . . well, okay, with Dave's help, but still. I sincerely hoped I didn't sound like that when I talked to Rob—you know, all sugary sweet and babyish. I think if I did, Rob would have told me to knock it off already. I hoped so, anyway.

I don't know what Dave was thinking as we made our way along the shore. He was pretty quiet. It had been, I reflected, a big day for both him and Scott. I mean, they had gotten to meet a real live psychic, thwart some FBI agents, and blow up a van, all in one day. No wonder he wasn't very talkative. It was a lot to process.

I was having trouble processing some stuff of my own. The Rob thing, if you want the truth, bothered me a lot more than the whole thing where I managed to find a kid without catching forty winks first—especially considering the fact that I am a vital, independent woman who has no need of a man to make her feel whole. I mean, I said I'd call him, and he'd said *don't?* What kind of baloney was that? Is it my fault I have this very important career, and that sometimes I am forced to think first not of my own personal safety, but about the children? Couldn't he see that this wasn't about him, or even me, but a missing twelve-year-old, who, it's true, couldn't stop making fart jokes, but nevertheless didn't deserve to perish in the wilds of northern Indiana?

Of course, there was also the small matter of my having dragged poor Rob into all of this in the first place. I mean, he'd come all the way up here, and driven me all around Chicago, and helped me deal with Keely, just because I'd asked him to. And he hadn't expected anything at all in return. Not even a single lousy kiss.

And all he'd gotten for it was a pistol brandished at him by a member of the FBI.

I guess, when you took into account all of these facts, it wasn't any wonder he didn't want me to call him anymore.

But while this was perhaps the most personally troubling of the problems that were on my mind as we trudged toward Wolf Cave, it was by no means the only one. There was also, of course, the puzzling little matter of just how Dr. Alistair had found out about me. I didn't believe Pamela had told him. It was strange that he had known where I was that afternoon, when Pamela hadn't even known. I mean, I'm sure she suspected, but I hadn't discussed my plans concerning Keely Herzberg with her. I figured the less people who knew about it, the better.

So how had Dr. Alistair known?

Then the moonlight vanished as we moved from the lake's shore to the deeply wooded embankment where Wolf Cave was located. If I had thought the wet grass was bad, this was about ten times worse. The incline was really steep, and since it was mostly unused, there was no path to follow . . . just slick, wet ground cover, mostly mud and dead leaves. The others had no choice but to turn on their flashlights now, if we didn't want to break our necks tripping over some root, or something.

In spite of our efforts to approach the cave quietly, we must have made a considerable amount of noise—especially considering the fact that Ruth would *not* shut up about her stupid ankles. It was pretty quiet, that deep in the woods. There were crickets chirping, but for the first time since I'd arrived at the camp, no cicadas screamed. Maybe the rain had drowned them all.

So it couldn't have been all that hard for Shane to hear our approach.

Which might have explained why, when we

finally reached the mouth of Wolf Cave—just a dark spot under an outcropping of boulders, jutting from the side of the steep hill we'd just climbed—there was no sign of Shane. . . .

Well, unless you count the candy wrappers and empty boxes of Fiddle Faddle that lined the narrow entrance.

I borrowed Ruth's flashlight and shined it into the cave—really, the mouth was surprisingly small . . . only three feet high and maybe two feet wide. I did not relish squeezing through it, let me tell you.

"Shane," I called. "Shane, come out of there. It's me, Jess. Shane, I know you're in there. You left all this Fiddle Faddle out here."

There was a sound from within the cave. It was the sound of someone crawling.

Only the sound was going away from us, not coming closer.

"Let's just leave him in there," Ruth suggested. "The little jerk completely deserves it."

Scott seemed sort of shocked by her callousness. "We can't do that," he said. "What if he gets lost in there?"

Ruth's eyelashes fluttered behind the lenses of her glasses. "Oh, Scott," she cooed in that unnaturally sweet voice. "You're so right. I never thought of that."

Yuck.

"Maybe," Dave said, "there's another way in. You know, a wider side entrance. Most caves have more than one."

"Shane," I called into the cave. "Look, I'm sorry, okay? I'm sorry I didn't give Lionel a strike. I swear he's got one now, okay?"

No response. I tried again.

"Shane, everybody is really worried about you," I called. "Even Lionel missed you. Even the girls from Frangipani Cottage miss you. In fact, they miss you the most. They're holding a candlelight vigil for you right now. If you come out, we can panty-raid them while they're praying for you. Seriously. I'll even donate a pair of my own panties to the cause."

Nothing. I straightened up.

"I'm going to have to go in there after him," I said softly.

"I'll go with you," Dave volunteered. Which was pretty gallant of him, if you think about it. But I suppose he was only doing it because he felt guilty over letting Shane slip away from him in the first place.

My gaze flicked over him. "You'll never fit."

Which was true. The only person small enough, of the four of us, to fit through that hole was me, and they all knew it.

"Besides," I said. "This is between me and Shane. I better go on my own. You guys stay here and make sure he doesn't sneak out any of those side entrances you were talking about."

Nobody needed to tell Ruth twice to stay put. She plunked down onto a nearby boulder and immediately began rubbing her chigger-ravaged ankles.

Scott and Dave offered me a couple of caving tips from their days as Cub Scouts—if you shine your flashlight into a hole, and can't see the bottom of it, that's a hole you should avoid.

Armed with this piece of information, I dropped down to my knees and began to crawl. It was no easy task, crawling on all fours and trying to see where I was going at the same time. Still, I managed not to fall down any bottomless holes. At least, not right away. Instead, I found myself inching along a narrow—but dry, at least—tunnel. There were, much to my gratification, no bats and nothing slimy. Just a lot of dried leaves, and the occasional scrunched Dorito.

One thing you had to hand to Shane: if it was attention he was after, he sure knew how to get it. His camp counselor was crawling through a hole in the ground after him, following his trail of Snicker bar wrappers and cookie crumbs. What more could a kid ask?

Still, the deeper I went, the more I thought he might be taking things a little far. I called out to Shane a few times, but the only response I heard was more scraping of jeans against rock. For a chubby kid, Shane sure could crawl fast.

There was no way to tell how deep we'd gone—a quarter of a mile? half?—into the earth before I noticed the cave was starting to widen a bit. Now I glimpsed stalactites, and what I knew from sixth grade bio were stalagmites—stalactites point down from the ceiling, while stalagmites shot up from the ground (stalactite, ceiling; stalagmite, ground. That's how Mr. Hudson explained it, anyway). Both, I remembered, were formed by the precipitation of calcite, whatever that was. Which meant, of course, that the cave wasn't as snug and dry as it seemed.

Not that I minded. That meant there'd be less chance of encountering any woodland creatures who might otherwise have chosen to make their home here, which suited me fine.

Soon the cave started widening. Eventually, it was big enough for me actually to stand up. As the way widened, I found myself in a cavern about the size of my room back home.

Only, unlike my room back home, it was filled with creepy shadows, and a floor that seemed to slope up toward the ceiling at the sides. Pointy stalactites loomed everywhere, and even when you shined your flashlight on them, you couldn't tell if they were hiding some bats, or if the stuff growing at their base was just a fungus or what.

I learned something that night. I really don't like caves too much. And I don't think I'll be telling the story of Paul Huck again to young and impressionable children when there happens to be a cave nearby.

Fortunately, Shane seemed as creeped out by the shadowy room as I was, since, even though there were several other tunnels opening out from it, he hadn't budged. The beam from my flashlight soon crossed his, and I studied him as he sat in his

Wranglers and his blue- and red-striped shirt, glaring at me.

"You're a damned liar," was the first thing he said to me.

"Oh, yeah?" There was an eerie echo in the cavern. Somewhere water was dripping, a steady *plink, plink, plink.* It appeared to be coming from one of the wider tunnels off the chamber we were in. "That's a nice thing to say to somebody who just crawled into the bowels of the earth to find you."

"How'd you know where to look?" Shane demanded. "Huh? How'd you know I'd be in the cave?"

"Easy," I said, sauntering over to him. "Everyone knows you took that Paul Huck story way too seriously."

"Bullshit!" Shane's voice bounced off the walls of the cave, his *bullshit* repeating itself over and over until it finally faded away.

I blinked at him. "Excuse me?"

"You used your powers to find me," Shane hollered. "Your psychic powers! You still have them. Admit it!"

I stopped coming toward him. Instead, I shined my flashlight on his face, picking up cookie crumbs and a Dorito-orange mouth.

"Shane," I said. "Is that what this was about? Getting me to prove I still have ESP?"

"Of course." Shane wiggled his butt against the hard cave floor, his lip curled disgustedly. "Why else? I knew you were lying about it. I knew the minute I saw that kid's picture in your hand, that first night. You're a liar, Jess. You know that? You can give me all the strikes you want, but the truth is, you're no better than me. Worse, maybe. Because you're a liar."

I narrowed my eyes at him. The kid was a piece of work.

"Oh, yeah," I said. "And you're one to talk. Do you have any idea how many people are out there looking for you? They all think you drowned in the lake."

"Too bad they didn't ask you, huh, Jess?" Shane's eyes were very bright in my flashlight's beam. "You could have set them straight, huh?"

"Your mom," I went on. "Your dad. They're probably worried sick."

"Serve them right," Shane said in a sullen tone. "Making me come to this stinking camp in the first place."

I crossed the rest of the distance between us, then sank down beside Shane, leaning my back against the hard stone wall.

"You know what, Shane?" I said. "I think you're a liar, too."

Shane made an offended sound. Before he could say anything else, I went on, not looking at him, but at the weird shadows across the way.

"You know what I think?" I said. "I think you like playing the flute. I don't think you'd be able to play that well if you didn't like it. You may have perfect pitch and all of that, but playing like that, that takes practice."

Shane started to say something, but I just kept on going.

"And if you really hated it that much, you wouldn't practice. So that makes you as big a liar as I am."

Shane protested, quite colorfully, that this was untrue. His use of four-letter words was really very creative.

"You want to know why I tell people I can't do the psychic thing anymore, Shane?" I asked him, when I got tired of listening to him sputter invectives. "Because I didn't like my life too much back when they all thought I could still do it. You know? It was too . . . complicated. All I wanted was to be a normal girl again. So that's why I started lying."

"I'm not a liar," Shane insisted.

"Okay," I said. "Let's say you aren't. My question to you would be, why aren't you?"

He just stared at me. "W-what?"

"Why aren't you lying? If you hate coming here to Lake Wawasee so much, why don't you just tell everyone you can't play anymore, same way I told everyone I can't find people anymore?"

Shane blinked a few times. Then he laughed uncertainly. "Yeah, right," he said. "That'd never work."

I shrugged. "Why not? It worked for me. You're

the only one who knows—outside of a few close friends—that I've still got this 'gift' of mine. Why can't you do the same thing? Just play bad."

Shane stared at me. "Play bad?"

"Sure. It's easy. I do it every year when our orchestra teacher holds chair auditions. I play badly—just a little badly—on purpose, so I don't get first chair."

Shane did a surprising thing then. He looked down at his hands. Really. Like they weren't attached to him. He looked down at them as if he were seeing them for the first time.

"Play bad," he whispered.

"Yeah," I said. "And then go out for football. If that's what you really want. Personally, I think giving up the flute for football is stupid. I mean, you can probably do both. But hey, it's your life."

"Play bad," he murmured again.

"Yeah," I said again. "It's easy. Just say to them, Yes, I *had* a gift. But then I lost it. Just like that." I snapped my fingers.

Shane was still gazing down at his hands. May I add that those hands—those hands that had made that achingly sweet music—were not too clean? They were grimy with dirt and potato chip crumbs.

But Shane didn't seem to care. "I had a gift," he murmured. "But then I lost it."

"That's it," I said. "You're getting the hang of it."

"I *had* a gift," Shane said, looking up at me, his eyes bright. "But then I lost it."

"Right," I said. "It will, of course, be a blow to

music-lovers everywhere. But I'm sure you'll make a very excellent receiver."

Shane's look of appreciative wonder turned to one of disgust. "Lineman," he said.

"I beg your pardon. Lineman."

Shane continued to stare at me. "Jess," he said. "Why did you come looking for me? I thought you hated me."

"I do not hate you, Shane," I said. "I wish you would stop picking on people who are smaller than you are, and I would appreciate it if you would stop calling me a lesbian. And I can guarantee, if you keep it up, someday someone is going to do something a lot worse to you than what Lionel did."

Shane just stared at me some more.

"But I do not," I concluded, "hate you. In fact, I decided on my way over here that I actually like you. You can be pretty funny, and I really do think you'll be a good football player. I think you'd be good at anything you set your mind to being."

He blinked at me, his chubby, freckled cheeks smudged with dirt and chocolate.

"Really?" he asked. "You really think that?"

"I do," I said. "Although I also think you need to get a new haircut."

He pulled on the back of his mullet and looked defensive. "I like my hair," he said.

"You look like Rod Stewart," I informed him.

"Who's Rod Stewart?" he wanted to know.

But this seemed beyond even my descriptive ability at that particular moment. So I just said, "You know what? Never mind. Let's just go back to the cabin. This place is giving me the major creeps."

We turned back toward the way we'd come. Which was when I noticed something.

And that's that we were not alone.

"Well, lookie what we have here," said Clay Larsson.

CHAPTER

16

I would just like to take this opportunity to say that I, for one, had not believed Special Agents Johnson and Smith when they'd announced that Mrs. Herzberg's boyfriend was on some kind of killing rampage, and that I was his next intended victim. I think I was pretty much under the impression that they were just trying to scare me, to get me alone with them somewhere so that they could make their observations of me without interruption.

For instance, had I gone with them to the Holiday Inn, Special Agent Smith would have undoubtedly gotten up very early and then sat there, with pen poised on notepad, at my bedside, to see if I'd wake up babbling about where Shane was, thus proving that I had lied about having lost my telekinetic powers, or whatever.

That's what a part of me had thought. I had

never—unlike Rob—taken very seriously the idea that there might be a man unhappy enough with my recent behavior to want me, you know. Dead.

At least, I didn't believe it until he was standing in front of me, with one of those long, security-guard-type flashlights in his hands. . . .

One of those flashlights that would actually make a really handy weapon. Like if you wanted to conk somebody over the head with it. Someone who, for example, had kicked you in the face earlier that day.

"Thought you'd seen the last of me, dincha, girlie?" Clay Larsson leered down at Shane and me. He was what you'd call a large man, though I couldn't say much for his fashion sense. He looked no prettier now, in the glow of my flashlight, than he'd looked in broad daylight.

And he was even less appealing now that he had the imprint of the bottom of my Puma tattooed across the bridge of his nose. There were deep purple and yellow scars around his eyes—bruising from the nasal cartilage I'd crushed with my kick—and his nostrils were crusted over with blood.

These were, of course, the unavoidable consequences of being kicked in the face. I couldn't really hold the contusions against him, fashion-wise. It was the razor stubble and the halitosis that he really could have done something about.

"Look," I said, stepping in front of Shane. "Mr. Larsson, I can appreciate that you might be upset with me."

It might interest you to know that, at this point,

my heart wasn't beating fast or anything. I mean, I guess I was scared, but usually, in situations like this, I don't tend to realize it until the whole thing is over. Then, if I'm still conscious, I usually throw up, or whatever.

"But you have to understand"—as I spoke, I was backing up, pushing Shane slowly toward one of the other tunnels that branched out from the cavern we were in—"I was only doing my job. I mean, you have a job, right?"

Looking at him, of course, I couldn't think what kind of moron might have hired him for any job. I mean, who would willingly employ anybody who gave so little thought to his personal grooming and hygiene? Look at his shirt, for Pete's sake: it was stained. Stained with what I really hoped was chili or barbecue sauce. It was certainly red, whatever it was.

But whatever: Clearly, a complete lack of adequate forethought had gone into Clay's ensemble, and I, for one, considered it a crying shame, since he was not, technically, an unattractive man. Maybe not a Hottie, but certainly Do-able, if you got him cleaned up.

"I mean, people call me up," I said, continuing to back up, "and they say their kid is missing or whatever, and I, well, what am I supposed to do? I mean, I have to go and get the kid. That's my job. What happened today was, I was just doing my job. You're not really going to hold that against me now, are you?"

He was moving slowly toward me, the beam from his flashlight trained on my face. This made it kind of hard for me to see what he was doing, other than inexorably coming at me. I had to shield my eyes with one hand, while, with the other, I kept pushing Shane back.

"You made Darla cry," Clay Larsson said in his deep, really quite menacing voice.

Darla? Who the heck was Darla?

Then it hit me.

"Yes," I said. "Well, I'm sure Mrs. Herzberg was quite upset." I wanted to point out to him that I had it on pretty good authority that he, in fact, had probably made Keely's mother cry a lot more often than I had—throwing bottles at people tends to do that— but I felt at this juncture in our conversation, it might not be the wisest thing to bring up.

"But the fact is," I said instead, "you two shouldn't have taken Keely away from her father. The court awarded him custody for a reason, and you didn't have any right to—"

"And"—Clay didn't seem to have heard my pretty speech—"you broke my nose."

"Well," I said. "Yes. I did do that. And you know, I'm really sorry about it. But you did have hold of my leg, remember? And you wouldn't let go of it, and I guess, well, I got scared. You aren't going to hold a grudge against me for that, are you?"

Evidently, he had every intention of doing so, since he said, "When I'm through with you, girlie, you're gonna have a new definition for scared."

Definition. Wow. A four-syllable word. I was impressed.

"Now, Mr. Larsson," I said. "Let's not do anything you might regret. I think you should know, this place is crawling with Feds. . . ."

"I saw 'em." I couldn't see his expression because of the light shining in my eyes, but I could hear his tone. It was mildly ironic. "Runnin' toward that burning van. Right before I saw you and your friends outside." He seemed to be grinning. "I was glad when I saw you were the one who went in."

"Oh, yeah?" I didn't know what else to say. Keep him talking, was all I could think to do. Maybe Ruth or one of the boys would hear him, and run for help. . . .

That is, if we weren't too deep underground for them to hear us.

"I like caves," Clay Larsson informed me. "This is a real nice one. Lots of different ways in. But only one way out . . . for you, anyway."

I did not like the sound of that.

"Now, Mr. Larsson," I said. "Let's talk this over, okay? I—"

"Couldn't have picked a better place for what I got planned if you'd tried," Clay Larsson finished for me.

"Oh," I said, gulping. My throat, which had been having a tendency lately, I noticed, to run a little on the dry side, felt like the Sahara. Oh, yeah, and remember how I said my heart wasn't beating fast?

Well, it was. Fast and hard.

"Um," I said. "Okay." I tried to remember what I'd learned in counselor training about conflict resolution. "So what I hear you saying, Mr. Larsson, is that you are unhappy with the way I took Keely from you—"

"And kicked me in the face."

"Right, and kicked you in the face. I hear you saying that you are somewhat dissatisfied with this turn of events—"

"You hear that correctly," Clay Larsson assured me.

"And what *I* would like to say to you"—I tried to keep my voice pleasant, like they'd said to in counselor training, but it was hard on account of how hard I was shaking—"is that this disagreement seems to be between you and me. Shane here really had nothing to do with it. So if it's all right with you, maybe Shane could just slip on out—"

"And run for those Fed friends of yours?" Clay Larsson's tone was as disgusted as mine had been pleasant. "Yeah. Right. No witnesses."

I swallowed hard. Behind me, I could feel Shane's breath, hot and fast, on the back of my arm. He was clinging to the belt loops of my jeans, strangely silent, for him. I wouldn't have minded a reassuring belch, but none seemed forthcoming. Under the circumstances, I regretted the crack I'd made about his hair.

Could I stall long enough to get Shane into a position so he could make it through one of those tunnels and escape? The opening I'd followed him through was way too narrow for Clay Larsson to fit into. If I could just distract him long enough . . .

"This isn't," I pointed out, "the way to go about ensuring that Mrs. Herzberg gets visitation rights, you know. I mean, a court of law would probably look askance at her sharing a household with a guy who had, um, attempted murder."

Clay Larsson asked, "Who said anything about attempted?"

And suddenly, the light that had been in my eyes danced crazily against the ceiling as Clay Larsson lifted the flashlight, with the intention, I supposed, of bringing it down on my head.

I screamed, "Run!" to Shane, who wasted no time doing so. He popped through the narrow tunnel behind us quicker than anybody in *Alice in Wonderland* had ever plunged down a rabbit hole. One minute he was there, and the next he was gone.

It seemed to me like following him would be pretty smart. . . .

But first I had to deal with this heavy flashlight coming at me.

Being small has its compensations. One of them is that I'm fast. Also, I can compress myself into spaces otherwise unfit for human occupation. In this case, I ducked behind this stalactite/stalagmite combo that had made a sort of calcite pillar to one side of the hole Shane had slipped through. As a result, Clay Larsson's flashlight connected solidly with the rock formation, instead of with my head.

There was an explosion of stone shards, and Clay Larsson said a very bad word. The calcite formation split in half, the stalactite plunging from the ceiling like an icicle off the gutter. It fell to the floor with a clatter.

As for me, well, I kept going.

Only along the way, somehow, I dropped my flashlight.

Considering what happened next, this might have been for the best. Clay, seeing the bright white beam, swung his own flashlight—with enough force for it to make a whistling noise as it sailed through the air—in the direction he thought I was standing. There was another loud clatter, this one from his heavy metal flashlight as it connected with the cavern wall.

He hadn't been kidding about the attempted murder thing. If that had been my head, I thought, with a touch of queasiness, I'd have a handy space near my brain stem right about now to keep loose change.

"Nice trick," Clay grunted, as he squatted down to retrieve my flashlight. "Only now you can't see to get out of here, can you, girlie?"

Good point. On the other hand, I could see what mattered most, and that was him.

And, more to the purpose, he couldn't see me. I figured I'd better press that advantage while I still had it.

The question was, how? I figured I had several options. I could simply stay where I was, until the inevitable moment I was once again caught in the sweeping arc of his flashlight . . . and now he had two flashlights, so make that two sweeping arcs.

My second option was to attempt to follow, as

quickly as I could, Shane down his rabbit hole. The only problem with this plan was that any rock I happened to kick loose on my way there would give me away. Could I really outcrawl a guy that size? I didn't think so.

My third alternative was the one I liked the least, but which seemed to be the one I was stuck with. So long as the guy had me to worry about, he wasn't going to mess with Shane. The longer I could keep him from trying to go after the kid, the better Shane's chances of somehow escaping.

And so it was, with great regret, that I made a sound to distract Clay, luring him toward where I hid, and away from Shane.

What I had not counted on was Clay Larsson being smart enough—and let's face it, sober enough—to fake me out. Which was exactly what he did. I'd thrown a pebble one way, thinking he'd follow the sound, and immediately darted in the opposite direction. . . .

Only to find, to my great surprise, that Mr. Larsson had whipped around and, fast as a cat, blocked my path.

I threw on the brakes, of course, but it was too late.

Next thing I knew, he'd tackled me.

As I went flying through the air, narrowly missing several stalactites, I had time to reflect that really, Professor Le Blanc was right: I *had* been lazy, never learning to read music. And I swore to myself that if I got out of Wolf Cave alive, I would dedicate the rest of my life to combating musical illiteracy.

I hit the floor of the cave with considerable force, but it was Clay Larsson's heavy body, slamming into mine, that drove all the wind from me. It also convinced me that moving again would probably be excessively painful—quite possibly even fatal, due to the massive internal injuries I was pretty sure I'd just incurred. As I lay there, dazed from the blow—which felt as if it had broken every bone in my body—I had time to wonder if they would ever find our skeletal remains, or if Shane and I would just be left to rot in Wolf Cave until the next camper, some other Paul Huck wannabe, stumbled across us.

This was a depressing thought. Because, you know, there were a lot of things I'd wanted to do that I'd never gotten a chance to. Buy my own Harley. Get a mermaid tattoo. Go to prom with Rob Wilkins (I know it's geeky, but I don't care: I think he'd look hot in a tux). That kind of stuff.

And now I was never going to get to.

So when Clay Larsson went, "Nightie-night, girlie," and raised his steel flashlight high in the air, I was more or less resigned to my death. Dying, I felt, would actually be a relief, as it would make the mind-numbing pain I felt in every inch of my body go away.

But then something happened that didn't make any sense at all. There was a thud, accompanied by a sickening, crunching noise—which I, as a veteran fistfighter, knew only too well was the sound of breaking bone—and then Clay Larsson's heavy body came slamming into mine again. . . .

Only this time, it appeared to be because the man was unconscious.

Suddenly recovering my mobility, I reached for his flashlight, which had fallen harmlessly to one side of my head, and shined it in the direction from which I'd heard the thudding sound. . . .

And there stood Shane, holding on to one end of the stalactite that had broken off from the cave ceiling, which he had clearly just swung, baseball-bat style, at Clay Larsson's head. . . .

And hit it out of the park.

Shane, looking down at Clay's limp, still form sprawled across my legs, dropped the stalactite, then glanced toward me.

I went, "Way to go, slugger."

Shane burst into tears.

CHAPTER

17

"**W**ell," I said. "What was I supposed to think? I mean, after that whole don't-call-me thing."

Rob, sounding—as usual—half-amused and half-disgusted with me, said, "I knew what you were after, Mastriani. You wanted to get rid of me so you could ditch the Feds and go after the little guy."

Shane—who was tucked into the bed beside mine in the Camp Wawasee infirmary, a thermometer in his mouth—made a noise that I suppose was meant to signal his objection to being called a little guy.

"Sorry," Rob said. "I meant little dude."

"Thank you," Shane said sarcastically.

"No talking," the nurse admonished him.

"And you were okay with that?" I asked Rob. "I mean, letting me ditch the Feds, and you, in order to go after Shane?"

I suppose it was kind of weird, the two of us

working out our recent relationship difficulties while the camp nurse fussed over me and Shane. But what else were we supposed to talk about? My recent brush with death? The expressions Ruth, Scott, and Dave had worn when Shane and I, bruised and battered, crawled out of Wolf Cave and asked them to call the police? The look on Rob's face when he'd roared up a minute or so later and heard what had happened in his absence?

"Of course I wasn't okay with that." Rob paused while the nurse butted in to take my pulse. Seemingly pleased by the steadiness of its beat, she moved away to do the same to Shane.

"But what was I supposed to do, Mastriani?" Rob went on. "The guy pulled a gun on me. Not like I thought he'd shoot me, but it was clear nobody—most specifically you—wanted me around."

I said defensively, "That isn't true. I always want you around."

"Yeah, but only if I'll go along with whatever harebrained idea you've come up with. And let me tell you, going into a cave in the middle of the night with a killer on the loose? Not one I'd probably go for."

I said, "Well, it all turned out okay."

Rob snorted. "Oh, yeah. Shane?" He turned around and looked at the chubby-cheeked boy in the bed next door. "You agree with that? You think it all turned out okay?"

Shane nodded vigorously. Then, when the nurse reached down and took the thermometer from his mouth, he said, "I think it turned out great."

Rob snorted. "You didn't seem to think so when you first got out of that cave."

Well, that much was true, anyway. Shane had pretty much been in hysterics up until Special Agents Smith and Johnson arrived, along with the sheriff and his deputies, and put a still unconscious Clay Larsson under arrest. They had a hard time dragging him out of that cave, believe me, even using the wider side entrance he'd discovered.

"Yeah," Shane admitted. "But that was before the cops got there. I was afraid he was going to wake up and come after us again."

"After that whack you gave him?" Rob raised his eyebrows. "Never mind football, kid. You've got batting in your blood."

Shane flushed with pleasure at this praise. He had nothing but admiration for Rob, having recognized him as the guy from the story I'd told that first night, the one about the murdering car.

What's more, Rob had pretty much been the only one who'd kept his head in the wake of our crawling out of Wolf Cave. That week's worth of counselor training hadn't prepared Ruth, Scott, or Dave for dealing with a couple of victims of an attempted murder.

"You know, Mastriani," Rob went on, "you have more than just an anger-management problem. You are also the stubbornest damned person I've ever met. Once you get an idea into your head, nothing can make you change your mind. Not your friends. Not the FBI. And certainly not me." He added, "I used to have a dog a lot like you."

This seemed to me to be neither flattering nor very romantic, but Shane found it hilarious. He giggled.

"What happened?" Shane wanted to know. "To the dog that was like Jess?"

"Oh," Rob said. "He was convinced he could stop moving cars with his teeth, if he could just sink them into their tires. Eventually, he got run over."

"I am not," I declared, "a car-chasing dog. Okay? There is absolutely no parallel between me and a dog that's stupid enough to—"

I broke off, realizing with indignation that Rob was chuckling to himself. He was in a much better mood now than he'd been earlier, when he hadn't been sure I wasn't seriously injured. He'd had a lot to say, let me tell you, on the subject of my insisting on staying at Camp Wawasee in order to find Shane, and thus endangering not only my life, but, as it had ended up, a lot of other people's as well.

And, of course, he was right. I'd screwed up. I was willing to admit it.

But, hey, things had turned out all right in the end.

Well, for everybody but Clay Larsson.

"So," I couldn't help asking, "you're not mad at me?"

All he said in reply was, "I think I'll be able to get over it."

But for Rob, that was like admitting—I don't know. His undying love for me, or something. So while I lay there, waiting for the inevitable moment when the nurse was going to decide I was well enough for questioning, I perked up. Why, I thought to myself, I'm going into my junior year! Juniors at Ernie Pyle High are allowed to go to the prom. I could invite Rob, and then I'd get to see him in a tux after all . . . that is, if he'd go with me. It *is* kind of weird, I'll admit, to go to prom with a guy who's already graduated, and who knows, maybe if I ask him, he'll refuse. . . .

But by the time prom rolls around, I'll finally be seventeen, so how *can* he refuse? I mean, really? Resist me? I don't think so.

These happy thoughts were somewhat dampened by the fact that Shane was in the next bed making gagging noises over what he deemed our "mushiness"—though if you ask me, there'd been nothing mushy at all going on . . . at least, not by *Cosmo* standards. Or any other standards, really, that I could see.

It was at that moment that the nurse went, "Well, from the sound of it, you two are well enough to take on a few more visitors. And there are a lot of them out there. . . ."

And then the evening became a blur of relieved faces and pointed questions, which we answered according to the story we'd so carefully prepared, Rob and Ruth and Scott and Dave and me, while we'd been waiting for the cops to show up.

"So," Special Agent Johnson said, sinking into a seat close to the one Rob occupied. "Anything you'd like to add to your somewhat sketchy account of just what, exactly, happened out there tonight, Miss Mastriani?"

I pretended to think about it. "Well," I said. "Let me see. I remembered a ghost story I'd told about a cave, so I figured I'd check the one on the camp property for Shane, just in case, and while we were in there, that crazy Larsson guy tried to kill us, and Shane whacked him in the head with a stalactite. That's about it, I think."

Special Agent Johnson didn't look very surprised. He looked over at Shane, who was sitting up in bed, fingering a plastic sheriff's badge one of the deputies had given him for his bravery.

"That sound right to you?"

Shane shrugged. "Yeah."

"I see." Special Agent Johnson closed his notebook, then exchanged a significant look with his partner, who was sitting on the end of my bed. "A hero. And just how, precisely, did you happen upon the scene, Mr. Wilkins? It was my impression that you left the camp some hours ago."

"Well," Rob said. "That's true. I did. But I came back."

"Uh-huh," Special Agent Johnson said. "Yes, I can see that. Any particular reason you came back?"

Rob did something very surprising then. He reached out, took hold of my hand, and said, "Well, I couldn't leave things the way they were with my girl, could I? I had to come back and apologize."

His girl? He had called me his girl! He had taken my hand and called me his girl!

I was grinning so happily, I was afraid my lips might break. Special Agent Johnson, noticing this, looked pointedly toward the ceiling, clearly sickened by my adolescent enthusiasm. But how could I help it? Rob had called me *his girl!* So what if he'd done it to throw off a federal investigation into my affairs that evening? Prom had never seemed so likely a prospect as it did at that moment.

"Um," Special Agent Johnson said. "I see. Please forgive me if I sound unconvinced. The fact is, Special Agent Smith and I feel that it is a bit of a co-incidence, Jess, that you went looking for young Master Shane in Wolf Cave. You certainly didn't mention that he might have been in this cave to any-one when you first learned of his disappearance."

"Excuse me, sir." The nurse appeared and stuck a mug of extremely hot, extremely sugary tea in my hands. "For the shock," she said in an explanatory manner to the agents, even though they hadn't asked, before she handed a similar mug to Shane.

I took a sip. It was surprisingly restorative, in spite of the fact that I was trying to look like someone whose only recent shock had been finding her boyfriend's tongue in her mouth.

Yeah, I know. Wishful thinking, right?

"Jess," Special Agent Smith said. "Why don't you tell us what really happened?"

I sat there, enjoying the warm tea flowing down my insides, and the warm arm flung across my out-sides. Talk about a happy camper.

"I already told it," I said, "exactly like it was."

At their raised eyebrows, I added, "No, really. That's it."

"Yes," Shane said. "She's telling the truth, sir."

We all looked over at Shane, who, like me, was downing his own mug of tea. He had, through it all, clung to his bag of Chips Ahoy cookies, and now he slipped one from the bag, and dunked it into his tea.

Special Agent Johnson looked back at me.

"Nice try," he said. "But I don't think so."

"I highly doubt, for instance," Special Agent Smith said, "that that little boy was the one who set off a Molotov cocktail beneath our van."

I rolled my eyes. "Well, obviously," I said, "that could only have been Mr. Larsson."

Both Special Agents Johnson and Smith stared down at me.

"No, really," I said. "To distract you. I mean, come on. The guy's a real psycho. I hope they put him away for a long, long time. Going after a little kid like that? Why, it's unconscionable."

"Unconscionable," Special Agent Johnson repeated.

"Sure," I said defensively. "That's a word. I took the PSATs. I should know."

"Funny how," Special Agent Johnson said, "Clay Larsson happened to know exactly which vehicle was ours."

"Yeah," I said, swallowing a sip of tea. "Well, you know. Criminal genius and all."

"And strange," Special Agent Smith said, "that he would pick our vehicle, out of all the other ones parked in that lot, to set on fire, when he doesn't even know us."

"One of the hardest things to accept," Rob remarked, "about violent crime is its seeming randomness."

They both looked at Rob, and I felt a moment of pride that I was, as he'd so matter-of-factly put it, his girl.

Then Dr. Alistair appeared at the end of my cot, wringing his hands.

"Jessica," he said, glancing worriedly from me to Special Agents Johnson and Smith and then back again. "You're all right?"

I looked at him like he was crazy. Which I was pretty sure he was.

"Oh, thank goodness," he cried, even though I hadn't said anything in reply to his question. "Thank goodness. I do hope, Jessica, that you'll forgive me for my outburst earlier this evening—"

I said, "You mean when you asked me why I didn't get my psychic friends to help me find Shane?"

He swallowed, and darted another nervous look at the agents.

"Yes," he said. "About that. I didn't mean—"

"Yes, you did," I said. "You meant every word." I looked hard at Special Agents Johnson and Smith. "How much did you guys pay him, anyway, to report my every move to you?"

Jill and Allan exchanged nervous glances.

"Jessica," Special Agent Smith said. "What are you talking about?"

"It's so obvious," I said, "that he was your narc. I

mean, he scheduled that one o'clock appointment with me, and then when I didn't show up, he called you. That's how you knew I'd left the camp. You didn't have to sit outside by the gates and wait to see if I'd leave. You had someone working on the inside to spare you the trouble."

"That," Special Agent Johnson said, "is patently—"

"Oh, come on." I rolled my eyes. "When are you guys going to get it through your heads that you're going to have to find yourselves a new Cassandra? Because the truth is, this one's retired."

"Jessica," Dr. Alistair cried. "I would never in a million years compromise the integrity of this camp by accepting money for—"

"Aw, shut up," Shane snapped. I could see that his campaign to be kicked out of music camp had now entered high gear. I hadn't any doubt that the traumatic event in Wolf Cave was going to—for the time being, anyway—have a detrimental effect on his ability to play the flute.

Dr. Alistair, looking startled, did shut up, to everyone's surprise.

Special Agent Johnson leaned forward and said, in a low, rapid voice, "Jessica, we know perfectly well that Jonathan Herzberg asked you to find his daughter, and that you, in fact, did so. We also know that this evening, you again used your psychic powers to find Shane Taggerty. You can't go on with this ridiculous charade that you've lost your psychic powers any longer. We *know* it isn't true. We *know* the truth." He leaned back and regarded me menacingly.

"And it's only a matter of time," Special Agent Smith added, "before you'll be forced to admit it, Jess."

I digested this for a moment. And then I said, "Jill?"

Special Agent Smith looked at me questioningly. "Yes, Jess?"

"Are you a lesbian?"

After that, the nurse made everyone leave, on account of the fact she was worried Shane was going to make himself sick from laughing so hard.

CHAPTER

18

"**D**oug," I said, trailing one hand through the cool, silver water.

Ruth, sprawled across an inner tube a few feet from mine, gazed through the dark lenses of her sunglasses into the clear blue sky overhead. "Do-able," she said, after a moment.

"Agreed," I said. "What about Jeff?"

Ruth adjusted a strap on her bikini. After six weeks of salads, she had finally deemed herself svelte enough for a two-piece. "Do-able," she said.

"Agreed." I leaned my head back and felt the sun beat down on my throat. It was beating down on other places, as well. After several weeks of spending my afternoons floating across the mirrored surface of Lake Wawasee, I was the color of Pocahontas. I would look, I knew, exceptionally good at tonight's all-camp concert, at which I was playing the piece

Professor Le Blanc had despaired of me ever learning, except by imitation.

I didn't have to imitate anyone, though. I could read each and every note.

A shout wasn't enough to break the trance-like daze the sun had sent Ruth and me into, but it got our attention. We lifted our heads and looked toward shore. Scott and Dave were playing Frisbee with some of the campers. Scott waved at us, and Dave, distracted, missed a catch, and landed in the sand.

"Dave," I said.

"Do-able," Ruth said.

"Agreed. Scott," I said, watching as he dove to make a catch.

"Hottie," Ruth said. "Of course."

I raised my sunglasses and looked at her from beneath the lenses in surprise.

"Really? He used to be Do-able."

"He's *my* summer fling," she informed me. "If I say he's hot, he's hot."

I lowered my sunglasses. "Okay," I said.

"Besides," she said. "That whole thing with lighting the Feds' van on fire? That was kind of cool. You might have something with the whole dangerous-guy thing."

"Rob," I said, "is not dangerous."

"Please," Ruth said. "Any guy who drives a motorcycle as his main form of transportation is dangerous."

"Really? Is that better than a guy with a convertible?"

Ruth shrugged. "Sure."

Wow. I leaned back, digesting this. My dangerous boyfriend was driving up to watch me perform at the concert that night. So was my family. I wondered what would happen if I introduced Rob to my mother. Frankly, I couldn't picture my mother and Rob in the same room. It was going to be very—

I felt something brush against the hand I was trailing in the water. I screamed and yanked my fingers away, just as Ruth did the same thing.

Two snorkel-fitted heads popped up from beneath the water and promptly began laughing at us.

"Ha-ha," Arthur cried, pointing at me as he treaded water. "You screamed just like a girl!"

"Like a girl," Lionel echoed incoherently. He was laughing too hysterically to speak.

"Very funny," I said to them. "Why don't you two swim over to the deep area and get a cramp?"

"Yeah," Ruth said. "And don't bother calling for us, because we won't come fish you out."

"Come on, Lionel," Arthur said. "Let's go. These two are no fun."

The two heads promptly disappeared. I watched the ends of their snorkels slice the water's surface as they headed back to shore. The two had become fast friends, once Shane was out of the picture and Lionel no longer spent every waking moment in fear of being tortured.

As I'd predicted, Shane's ability to play the flute had mysteriously disappeared shortly after the Wolf Cave incident, and though it was too late to get him into any self-respecting football camp, several had offered him scholarships, based on his size alone, for the following summer. Mr. and Mrs. Taggerty were not, it was rumored, happy about this, but what could they do? The boy was, according to more than one coach, a natural.

Off over in the direction of Wolf Cave, a cicada began its shrill call—one of the last ones I'd hear, I knew, before they all sank back into the ground to hibernate until next summer.

"So did Dr. Alistair ask you to come back next year?" Ruth wanted to know.

"Yeah," I said, with some disgust. "I suppose so he can supplement his income again by ratting me out to the Feds."

"How'd you know it was him, anyway?" Ruth asked.

I shrugged. "I don't know. I just did. Same way I know they're still monitoring me."

Ruth nearly lost her balance in the inner tube. "They *are?*" she sputtered. "How do you know?"

I pointed out toward the trees on the side of the lake closest to us. "See that thing over there, glinting in the sun?"

Ruth looked where I was pointing. "No. Wait. Yeah. I guess. What is that?"

"Telephoto lens," I said, lowering my arm. "Watch. Now that he knows we spotted him, he'll drive to some other spot and try again."

Sure enough, the glint disappeared, and far off, we heard the sound of a car engine.

"Ew," Ruth cried. "How creepy! Jess, how can you stand it?"

I shrugged. "What can I do? That's just the way it is, I guess."

Ruth chewed her lower lip. "But aren't you . . . I mean, aren't you worried they're going to catch you one of these days? In a lie, I mean?"

"Not really." I tilted my head back, letting the sun warm my neck again. "The trick, I guess, is just never to stop."

"Never stop what?"

"Lying," I said.

"Isn't that going to be hard," Ruth asked, "now that . . . well, you know? Now that your powers are getting stronger?"

I shrugged. "Probably." It wasn't something I liked to think about.

"Hey," I said, to change the subject. "Isn't that Karen Sue over there, on that pink inflatable raft?"

Ruth looked, then made a face. "I can't believe she's wearing one of those headbands in the water. And is that Todd she's with? He is so not Do-able. Did you hear him rehearsing that piece he's playing tonight? Bartok. What a show-off."

"Let's go tip them over," I suggested.

"You've got to be kidding," Ruth said. "That's so . . ."

I raised my eyebrows. "So what?"

"So childish," Ruth said. Then she grinned. "Let's do it."

And so we did.

Jenny Carroll

Born in Indiana, Jenny Carroll spent her childhood in pursuit of air conditioning - which she found in the public library where she spent most of her time. She has lived in California and France and currently resides in New York City with her husband and a one-eyed cat named Henrietta. Jenny Carroll is the author of the hugely popular Mediator series as well as the bestselling Princess Diaries. Visit Jenny at her website, www.jennycarroll.com

Read Jenny Carroll's

the mediator

series in Pocket Books

A new school, annoying step-brothers and
disastrous first dates – these are nothing in
comparison to Susannah's other problems.
The ghostly hunk sitting in her new bedroom
and the psycho spirit haunting the locker
room who's out for revenge on her ex-
boyfriend – that's what Susannah calls real
trouble . . .

ISBN 07434 30506